the gift knitter

tara jon manning

PHOTOGRAPHS BY KATE BURTON

IB

BERKLEY BOOKS, NEW YORK

the gift knitter

knitting chunky
for babies
with four legs
and two

THE BERKLEY PUBLISHING GROUP
Published by the Penguin Group
Penguin Group (USA) Inc.
375 Hudson Street, New York, New York 10014, USA
Penguin Group (Canada), 10 Alcorn Avenue, Toronto, Ontario M4V 3B2, Canada
(a division of Pearson Penguin Canada Inc.)
Penguin Books Ltd., 80 Strand, London WC2R 0RL, England
Penguin Group Ireland, 25 St. Stephen's Green, Dublin 2, Ireland (a division of Penguin Books Ltd.)
Penguin Group (Australia), 250 Camberwell Road, Camberwell, Victoria 3124, Australia
(a division of Pearson Australia Group Pty. Ltd.)
Penguin Books India Pvt. Ltd., 11 Community Centre, Panchsheel Park, New Delhi—110 017, India
Penguin Group (NZ), Cnr. Airborne and Rosedale Roads, Albany, Auckland 1310, New Zealand
(a division of Pearson New Zealand Ltd.)
Penguin Books (South Africa) (Pty.) Ltd., 24 Sturdee Avenue, Rosebank, Johannesburg 2196, South Africa

Penguin Books Ltd., Registered Offices: 80 Strand, London WC2R 0RL, England

This book is an original publication of The Berkley Publishing Group.

Copyright © 2004 by Tara Jon Manning.
Original line drawings and illustrations by Tara Jon Manning .
Photographs by Kate Burton.
Technical editing by Lori Gayle.
Cover design by Rita Frangie.
Text design by Tiffany Estreicher.

PRINTING HISTORY
Berkley trade paperback edition / September 2004

Library of Congress Cataloging-in-Publication Data
Manning, Tara Jon, 1968–
    The gift knitter : knitting chunky for babies with four legs & two / Tara Jon Manning ;
with photographs by Kate Burton.
        p. cm.
    ISBN 0-425-19810-3
    1. Knitting—Patterns.   2. Infants' clothing.   3. Dogs—Equipment and supplies.   I. Title.
TT825.M173 2004
746.43'2043—dc22   2004049438

PRINTED IN THE UNITED STATES OF AMERICA

10   9   8   7   6   5   4   3   2   1

Dedicated to my little loves, with four legs and two—
Jack, Zane, Molly, Sammy, and Rosie.

Heartfelt thanks are extended to everyone who has been part of the creation of this project. Here are a few special names to include my thanks to:

. . . furry friends everywhere for unquestioned love and devotion—especially to Molly for her trust and patience (I know you can't read, but I'll read it to you).

. . . my dear family—Bill, Jack, and Zane.

. . . the manufacturers and distributors who graciously supplied the materials used for the projects in this book.

. . . Linda Roghaar and the Linda Roghaar Literary Agency for support and encouragement.

. . . Allison McCabe and Berkley Books for such a fun idea and the development and fruition of this project!

. . . Lori Gayle for her support, tender loving care of the patterns, extensive knowledge, and technical editing skill.

. . . Diane Carlson for contributing her fine knitting talents.

contents

introduction

picking up stitches

One spark that gets many people knitting is the impending arrival of a new family member. For some this means a new baby; for others their bundle of joy is of the four-legged variety. Knitting little things for little recipients is wonderful: Little things are cute, little things are quick, little things allow you to try new techniques and ideas without investing a lot of time or money in materials.

In this collection of playful designs for little friends—with four legs and two—you will find both funky and classic (but updated) designs. The projects are fun, easy, and quick to knit. Featuring very basic shapes, they

are knit in big gauges—from worsted weight to super bulky. The techniques and shapings are kept simple, so that newer knitters can embrace them, and longtime knitters can use them as a resource for quick gift projects. Consideration has been given to selecting yarns that are easy to care for, as baby clothes need to be washed often! Also, materials are stated in terms that make yarn substitutions easy. I encourage knitters to try something new with every project, so my patterns are supported by a detailed collection of knitting tips—a helpful reference to guide you through techniques you haven't tried yet.

So let's get knitting! The designs that follow are so fast and easy, you'll likely knit them over and over again in many variations and iterations, as you receive requests from family and friends for another, and another . . .

casting off tradition:
one-of-a-kind creativity

Every hand-knitted item is a unique, one-of-a-kind creation.

The projects in this collection are intended as blank canvases for your own whim and fancy. Throughout this book you will find helpful suggestions to encourage you to use your imagination to make everything you knit impressive. Even if you follow the same pattern over and over again, do try something new with every project. Something as simple as choosing a textured yarn can completely change the look of an item you've knitted many times before, and create a garment that specifically reflects the style and personality of the recipient.

when sticks click: gift knitting

What is "gift knitting"? For me, the garments I knit are tangible manifestations of goodwill, the work of my hands, physical evidence of time spent engaged in good thoughts and best wishes for those I love. The process of knitting these garments provides me with a means of creating beautiful, original gifts full of love and good intentions.

As we knit each stitch, we can find ourselves reflecting on our feelings for the person (or critter) for whom we are knitting. Every bit of fabric is then filled with love and blessings for the recipient. Every stitch becomes a physical marker of our affection. Our knitting is infused with our best intentions and the essence of those for whom we knit. In this way, knitting becomes the ultimate expression of our caring—a one-of-a-kind record of our thoughts, an expression of fondness and generosity.

When I begin a gift project, I fill myself with thoughts and reminiscences of the recipient. I think about the things that make them dear to me, I ponder our friendship, or remember kindnesses they have extended to me. When selecting the pattern and materials, I think about what color and style might make them look best, or what might make them smile. I consider when they are likely to use the garment: Will they wear it in cold weather or as an accessory? What yarn choice will be most convenient for them? Will it be worn frequently and require repeated washings or would something playful and less practical be more in tune with their style?

I have a dear friend, who, coincidentally, I met several years ago at a knitting group. When we met, we were each expecting our first child.

Those boys, now six years old, have become the "bestest" of friends. When she was expecting her second child, I simply had to make something for her new baby. I chose to make a cotton sweater in size 6–12 months, so the child could get a lot of wear out of it. A preshrunk cotton yarn provided easy care. Also, cotton provides the perfect weight for layering—an important component in dressing for Colorado weather. My friend and her husband chose not to learn the sex of the baby ahead of time—so I chose a soft, unisex green, and in the event of a girl, I planned to embroider a flower motif on the collar and cuffs. It turned out the flowers were not necessary, as this baby was a little boy. My friend is a very generous person and has made many lovely gift handknits for numerous friends and babies. When I presented the little sweater to her, tears welled up in her eyes; in all the years of making knitted things for others, it turns out no one had presented a hand-knitted gift to her for her kids. Perhaps they thought it would be like giving snow to an Eskimo? All I know is the appreciation expressed in her delight in receiving this gift was so touching, it was the greatest reward in and of itself. The ultimate gift.

Through the act of making things to give, we enjoy a sense of pride in our handwork, a great sense of accomplishment, and we watch our knitting skills grow. In knitting gifts, we can find delight in making someone feel special with a display of our love and time. We can offer a unique expression of appreciation in a very personal and meaningful way. As we create customized one-of-a-kind gift knits we impart our blessings to those we care about. We can literally give a "hug" that can be worn on a chilly day.

As you explore the projects in this collection, I encourage you to explore and develop your own understanding of your personal notions of generosity. Engaging in gift knitting allows your knitting time to be enhanced with a sense of cheerfulness as you find great joy in giving—giving a bit of yourself, your time, and your attention. As you partake in the acts of creating and giving, you will find that you will receive a most wonderful gift in return—the unspoken appreciation of our smallest loved ones: those who cannot thank you with words, but who thank you with the blessings of their presence in your life.

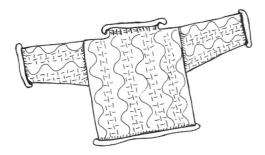

boy or purl?

KNITTING FOR BABIES

chunky jacket

a simple and classic silhouette—you'll be done with this fast-knitting little sweater so quickly you'll be making your second, and then your third, in no time. A cuddly gift, this project is perfect for the newer knitter who wants to explore the techniques needed to construct a garment—and the seasoned knitter who has a lot of pregnant friends! If you are making this as a gift and don't know the baby's gender, the Dutch blue sweater shown here can be unisex if you choose a neutral color such as yellow, sage green, natural, or red. I used a soft, lofty 100% wool with contrasting trim. For a "girlier" version, place buttonholes on right front, and also check out the Fancy Chunky Jacket on page 7.

FINISHED SIZE
To fit 6 (12, 24) months; shown in size 12 months.

FINISHED MEASUREMENTS
Chest circumference (buttoned): 22½ (25, 28)"; 57 (63.5, 71) cm

Length from bottom edge to shoulder: 9½ (13, 15)"; 24 (33, 38) cm

Sleeve length: 6½ (8, 8)"; 16.5 (20.5, 20.5) cm

MATERIALS
Yarn: 150 (250, 300) yards (140 [230, 275] meters) bulky weight yarn that knits to correct gauge in main color (MC); 30 yards (28 meters) of contrasting color for edging (CC).

Shown in Crystal Palace Labrador (100% wool; 90 yards [82 meters]/100 grams), #7063 Dutch blue (MC) and #5329 celadon (CC).

Needles: Size US 11 (8 mm) straight needles, or size to obtain gauge.

Notions: Five ⅞" (2.2-cm) buttons, measuring tape, yarn needle, scissors, four stitch holders, crochet hook size J/10 (6 mm).

Gauge: 12 sts and 18 rows = 4" (10 cm) in stockinette stitch (St st). Check your gauge before you begin.

special technique
two-row buttonhole
Row 1: (WS) Work 2 sts in patt, BO the next 2 sts, work to end of row.

Row 2: (RS) Work in patt to gap created by BO sts in previous row, CO 2 sts over gap using either a backward loop or knitting-on method (see page 102), work to end of row.

back
With MC, loosely CO 34 (38, 42) sts. Work even in stockinette stitch (St st) until piece measures 5 (7, 8)" (12.5 [18, 20.5] cm) from CO. Shape for armholes: BO 2 sts at beg of next 2 rows—30 (34, 38) sts. Work even until piece meas 9 (12½, 14½)" (23 [31.5, 37] cm) from CO. Shape for back neck: Work across 9 (10, 11) sts, join a separate ball of yarn, BO center 12 (14, 16) sts, work across rem 9 (10, 11) sts. Cont working both shoulders separately until total length meas 9½ (13, 15)" (24 [33, 38] cm) from CO. Place rem sts for each shoulder on a separate st holder.

right front
With MC, loosely CO 19 (21, 23) sts. Work even in St st until piece meas 5 (7, 8)" (12.5 [18, 20.5] cm) from CO, ending with a RS row. Shape for armhole: BO 2 sts at beg of next WS row, work to end—17 (19, 21) sts. Work even until piece meas 7½ (10½, 12¼)" (19 [26.5, 31] cm) from CO, ending with a WS row. Shape for neck: At beg of next RS row (neck edge), BO 6 (7, 7) sts, work to end—11 (12, 14) sts. Dec 1 st at neck edge every other row 2 (2, 3) times—9 (10, 11) sts. Work even until front meas 9½ (13, 15)" (24 [33, 38] cm) from CO, or same length as back. Place rem sts for shoulder on st holder.

left front
Work as for right front, reversing shaping by working armhole BO at the beg of a RS row, working neck

[handwritten notes:]

25 Front
-3 armhole
22
-8 neck
14
2 neck edge

Sleeves p.u. 19 / 18 / 37 sts along edge
dec. ea side ev. 2nd row
until 6" wide: 24 sts.

ont and back together with RS of fabric
WS of piece facing outward. With MC,
eedle bind-off technique (see page 108),
oulders. Join left shoulders in the same

I RS facing, using crochet hook to assist if
up 28 (36, 42) sts evenly beg and ending
le notches, including 1 st picked up from
e BO notch. Work in St st, dec to shape
: Dec 1 st each end of row every 4 rows 5
—18 (24, 28) sts. Work even in St st until
6½ (8, 8)" (16.5 [20.5, 20.5] cm) from

I n
the e
you dor
try an
edging
yarn
or text
tri
loc

shaping at th
and making
tonholes as fo

Using two-row buttonhole method
(see page 4), work 1st buttonhole
½" (1.3 cm) up from CO edge, then
work 4 more buttonholes spaced
approximately 1⅝ (2⅜, 2¾)" (4 [6,
7] cm) apart, with last buttonhole
about ½" (1.3 cm) below beg of
neck shaping. See the knitting tip
about Intuitively Placed Buttonholes on page 101. When left front
has been completed, place rem sts
for shoulder on st holder.

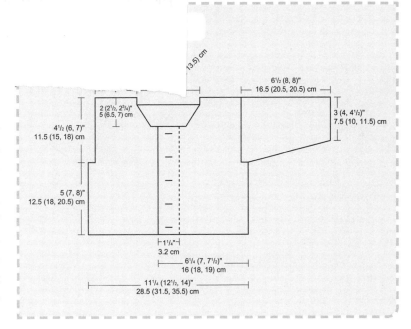

2 (2½, 2¾)"
5 (6.5, 7) cm

6½ (8, 8)"
16.5 (20.5, 20.5) cm

3 (4, 4½)"
7.5 (10, 11.5) cm

4½ (6, 7)"
11.5 (15, 18) cm

5 (7, 8)"
12.5 (18, 20.5) cm

1¼"
3.2 cm

6¼ (7, 7½)"
16 (18, 19) cm

11¼ (12½, 14)"
28.5 (31.5, 35.5) cm

13.5) cm

pickup row, or desired length. Loosely BO all sts. Repeat for other sleeve.

finishing

Sew sleeve and side seams. Weave in all ends on WS. Crochet edge: With RS facing, CC and crochet hook, beg at a side seam, work a row of single crochet around the bottom, front and neck edges, ending back where you started. Fasten off last st and weave in ends. Work a row of single crochet in the same manner around sleeve cuffs. Sew five buttons to right front to correspond with buttonholes on left front. Please attach your buttons very securely to keep the baby from pulling them off and putting them in his or her mouth.

fancy chunky jacket

also using big yarn on big needles, this fancy version of the fast-knitting Chunky Jacket features a beautiful, nubby-textured boucle yarn, giving it a very "Jackie O" feel—you'll have the little cutie knit up in no time. It is worked in reverse stockinette stitch to further play up the yarn's texture. After you make your first, and friends and family ask for more, think about trying different texture and fiber combinations. To create truly one-of-a-kind pieces, check your stash or your local yarn shop for inspiration. You might try knitting two yarns of different textures together for a really unique outcome.

special technique
two-row buttonhole
Row 1: (RS) Work 2 sts in patt, BO the next 2 sts, work to end of row.
Row 2: (WS) Work in patt to gap created by BO sts in previous row, CO 2 sts over gap using either a backward loop or the knitting-on method (see page 102), work to end of row.

back
Loosely CO 30 (34, 38) sts. Work even in reverse stockinette stitch (rev St st) until piece measures 5 (7, 8)" (12.5 [18, 20.5] cm) from CO. Shape for armholes: BO 2 sts at beg of next 2 rows—26 (30, 34) sts. Work even until piece meas 9 (12½, 14½)" (23 [31.5, 37] cm) from CO. Shape for back neck: Work across 8 (9, 10) sts, join a separate ball of yarn, BO center 10 (12, 14) sts, work across rem 8 (9, 10) sts. Cont working both shoulders separately until total length meas 9½ (13, 15)" (24 [33, 38] cm) from CO. Place rem sts for each shoulder on a separate st holder.

left front
Loosely CO 17 (19, 21) sts. Work even in rev St st until piece meas 5 (7, 8)" (12.5 [18, 20.5] cm) from CO, ending with a WS row. Shape for armhole: BO 2 sts at beg of next RS row, work to end—15 (17, 19) sts. Work even until piece meas 7½ (10½, 12¼)" (19 [26.5, 31] cm) from CO, ending with a RS row. Shape for neck: At beg of next WS row (neck edge), BO 5 (6, 6) sts, work to end—10 (11, 13) sts. Dec 1 st at neck edge every other row 2 (2, 3) times—8 (9, 10) sts. Work even until front meas 9½ (13, 15)" (24 [33, 38] cm) from CO, or same length as back. Place rem sts for shoulder on st holder.

right front
Work as for left front, reversing shaping by working armhole BO at the beg of a WS row, working neck

shaping at the beg of a RS row, and making 5 evenly spaced button-holes as foll:

Using two-row buttonhole method (see page 8), work 1st buttonhole ½" (1.3 cm) up from CO edge, then work 4 more buttonholes spaced approximately 1⅝ (2⅜, 2¾)" (4 [6, 7] cm) apart, with last but-tonhole about ½" (1.3 cm) below beg of neck shaping. See the knit-ting tip about Intuitively Placed Buttonholes on page 101. When right front has been completed, place rem sts for shoulder on st holder.

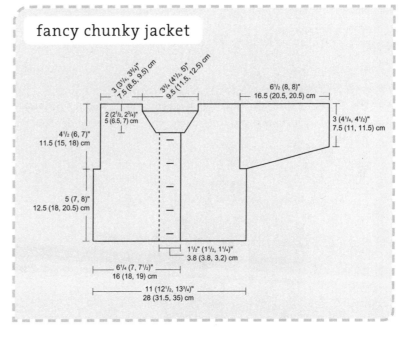

fancy chunky jacket

3 (3¼, 3¾)"
7.5 (8.5, 9.5) cm

3¾ (4½, 5)"
9.5 (11.5, 12.5) cm

6½ (8, 8)"
16.5 (20.5, 20.5) cm

2 (2½, 2¾)"
5 (6.5, 7) cm

3 (4¼, 4½)"
7.5 (11, 11.5) cm

4½ (6, 7)"
11.5 (15, 18) cm

5 (7, 8)"
12.5 (18, 20.5) cm

1½" (1½, 1¼)"
3.8 (3.8, 3.2) cm

6¼ (7, 7½)"
16 (18, 19) cm

11 (12½, 13¾)"
28 (31.5, 35) cm

Just as with the plain version of this jacket, you can play with different colors and techniques for the trim. Choose a coordinating solid to emphasize one of the colors found in your multicolor yarn; use an embroidered blanket stitch instead of single crochet—these details will make your simple sweater irreplaceable.

join shoulders

Hold right front and back together with RS of fabric touching and WS of piece facing outward. For this garment, the purl side is the right or "public" side of the fabric. Using three-needle bind-off technique (see page 108), join right shoulders. Join left shoulders in the same manner.

sleeves

With RS facing, using crochet hook to assist if desired, pick up 25 (33, 39) sts evenly beg and ending at the armhole notches, including 1 st picked up from each armhole BO notch. Work in rev St st, dec to shape sleeve as foll: Dec 1 st each end of row every 4 (4, 3) rows 4 (5, 7) times—17 (23, 25) sts. Work even in rev St st until sleeve meas 6½ (8, 8)" (16.5 [20.5, 20.5] cm) from pickup row, or desired length. Loosely BO all sts. Repeat for other sleeve.

finishing

Sew sleeve and side seams. Weave in all ends on WS (knit side of fabric). Crochet edge: With RS facing, and crochet hook, beg at a side seam, work a row of single crochet around the bottom, front and neck edges, ending back where you started. Fasten off last st and weave in ends. Work a row of single crochet in the same manner around sleeve cuffs. Sew five buttons to left front to correspond with buttonholes on right front. Please attach your buttons very securely to keep the baby from pulling them off and putting them in her mouth.

faux fur cardigan

CARDIGAN WITH TRIM

furry, fun, and funky are a few words to describe this playful little cardigan. A real showstopper, it is must-have for every hip baby girl. The sweater is simple to knit, and the easy-to-apply fur trim adds a pizzazz that belies the simple construction of this fashionable little piece, shown here in a classic red-and-black combination. Let your imagination run wild with different color and texture combinations and play up the funk!

FINISHED SIZE
To fit 6 (12, 24) months; shown in size 12 months.

FINISHED MEASUREMENTS
Chest circumference (buttoned): 20½ (25, 28½)"; 52 (63.5, 72.5) cm
Length from bottom edge to shoulder: 10½ (12½, 14½)"; 26.5 (31.5, 37) cm
Sleeve length: 7½ (8½, 10)"; 19 (21.5, 25.5) cm

MATERIALS
Yarn: 310 (425, 570) yards (285 [390, 520] meters) Aran weight wool that knits to correct gauge in main color (MC); 85 yards (78 meters) of contrasting fur-type yarn for edging (CC).

Shown in Mission Falls 1824 Wool (100% machine-washable Merino wool; 85 yards [78 meters]/50 grams), #011 poppy red (MC), and Crystal Palace Splash (100% polyester; 85 yards [78 meters]/100 grams) #0202 ebony (CC).
Needles: Size US 8 (5 mm) straight needles, or size to obtain gauge.
Notions: Five ⅝" (1.6-cm) buttons, measuring tape, yarn needle, scissors, four stitch holders, crochet hook size J/10 (6 mm).
Gauge: 18 sts and 24 rows = 4" (10 cm) in stockinette stitch (St st). Check your gauge before you begin.

special technique

yarnover buttonhole

Work buttonholes 2 sts away from the center front edge as foll: On RS rows, k2, k2tog, yo, work to end of row; on WS rows, work to last 4 sts, yo, p2tog, p2.

back

With CC, loosely CO 46 (56, 64) sts. Knit 2 rows. Change to MC and work even in stockinette stitch (St st) until piece measures 5½ (6½, 7½)" (14 [16.5, 19] cm) from CO. Shape for armholes: BO 2 sts at beg of next 2 rows—42 (52, 60) sts. Work even until piece meas 10¼ (12¼, 14¼)" (26 [31, 36] cm) from CO. Shape for back neck: Work across 12 (15, 18) sts, BO center 18 (22, 24) sts, work across rem 12 (15, 18) sts. Place rem sts for each shoulder on a separate st holder.

left front

With CC, loosely CO 26 (30, 34) sts. Knit 2 rows. Change to MC, and work even in St st until piece meas 5½ (6½, 7½)" (14 [16.5, 19] cm) from CO. Shape for armhole: BO 2 sts at beg of next RS row, work to end—24 (28, 32) sts. Work even until piece meas 6 (8, 10)" (15 [20.5, 25.5] cm) from CO, ending with a WS row. Shape for neck: Beg with the next RS row, dec 1 st at neck edge (end of RS rows, beg of WS rows) every other row 9 (8, 7) times, then every row 3 (5, 7) times—12 (15, 18) sts. Work even until front meas 10½ (12½, 14½)" (26.5 [31.5, 37] cm) from CO, or same length as back. Place rem sts for shoulder on st holder.

right front

Work as for left front, reversing shaping by working armhole BO at the beg of a WS row, working neck

This project provides a playful vehicle to explore some of the snazzy novelty yarns available on the market today. Consider using a multi-toned fur to kick it up a notch. You could even use a multicolored yarn for the main color of the sweater, and add coordinating solid fur to pull out your favorite tones. Furs and eyelash yarns come in so many different colors, textures, and lengths—there's no end to the creative combinations you can dream up to customize this super-fun little sweater.

shaping at beg of RS rows or end of WS rows, and making 5 evenly spaced buttonholes as foll:

Using yarnover buttonhole method (as before), work 1st buttonhole ½" (1.3 cm) up from CO edge, then work 4 more buttonholes spaced approximately 1¼ (1¾, 2¼)" (3.2 [4.5, 5.5] cm) apart, with last buttonhole about ½" (1.3 cm) below beg of neck shaping. See the knitting tip about Intuitively Placed Buttonholes on page 101. When right front has been completed, place rem sts for shoulder on st holder.

join shoulders

Hold right front and back together with RS of fabric touching and WS of piece facing outward. Using three-needle bind-off technique (see page 108), join right shoulders. Join left shoulders in the same manner.

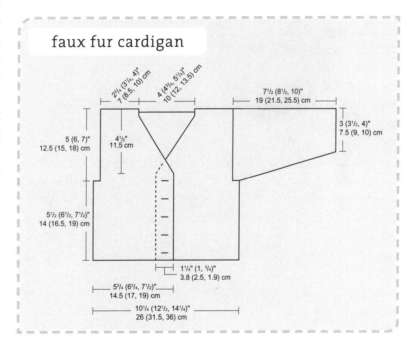

faux fur cardigan

2¼ (3¼, 4)"
7 (8.5, 10) cm

4 (4¾, 5¼)"
10 (12, 13.5) cm

7½ (8½, 10)"
19 (21.5, 25.5) cm

3 (3½, 4)"
7.5 (9, 10) cm

5 (6, 7)"
12.5 (15, 18) cm

4½"
11.5 cm

5½ (6½, 7½)"
14 (16.5, 19) cm

1¼" (1, ¾)"
3.8 (2.5, 1.9) cm

5¾ (6¾, 7½)"
14.5 (17, 19) cm

10¼ (12½, 14¼)"
26 (31.5, 36) cm

sleeves

With RS facing, using crochet hook to assist if desired, pick up 45 (55, 63) sts evenly beg and ending at the armhole notches, including 1 st picked up from each armhole BO notch. Work in St st, dec to shape sleeve as foll: Dec 1 st each end of row every 4 rows 9 (12, 14) times—27 (31, 35) sts. Work even in St st, if necessary, until sleeve meas 7 (8, 9½)" (18 [20.5, 24] cm) from pickup row, or ½" (1.3 cm) less than desired length, ending with a WS row. Change to CC and knit 2 rows. Loosely BO all sts. Repeat for other sleeve.

finishing

Sew sleeve and side seams. Weave in all ends on WS. Fur trim: With RS facing, crochet hook and CC, beg at the lower right front edge, pick up 106 (126, 146) sts evenly around front opening as foll: 26 (35, 44) sts along straight edge of right front, 18 sts along right V-neck shaping, 18 (20, 22) sts across back neck, 18 sts along left V-neck shaping, 26 (35, 44) sts along straight edge of left front. Knit 2 rows, then loosely BO all sts. Weave in ends. Sew five buttons to left front to correspond with buttonholes on right front. Please attach your buttons very securely to keep the baby from pulling them off and putting them in her mouth.

pawprints cardigan

knit in soft machine-washable Merino wool, this adorable sweater can be knit for little dog lovers of either gender. The super-cute pawprints are perfect practice for knitters new to intarsia, the technique of knitting a block of color into a solid background. If this sweater is a gift and you don't know the baby's gender, make the buttonholes as if for a boy to make it unisex. Pick neutral color combinations and let your imagination be your guide.

FINISHED SIZE
To fit 6 (12, 24) months; shown in size 6 months.

FINISHED MEASUREMENTS
Chest circumference (buttoned): 22½ (25, 27)"; 57 (63.5, 68.5) cm
Length from bottom edge to shoulder: 10 (12, 14)"; 25.5 (30.5, 35.5) cm
Sleeve length: 7½ (8½, 10)"; 19 (21.5, 25.5) cm

MATERIALS
Yarn: 310 (400, 525) yards (285 [365, 480] meters) Aran weight wool that knits to correct gauge in main color (MC); 50 (55, 60) yards (45 [50, 55] meters) of contrasting color for pawprints and trim (CC).
Shown in Mission Falls 1824 Wool (100% machine-washable Merino wool; 85 yards [78 meters]/50 grams), #016 thyme (MC) and #002 stone (CC).
Needles: Size US 8 (5 mm) straight needles, or size to obtain gauge.
Notions: Five ¾" (1.9-cm) buttons, measuring tape, yarn needle, scissors, four stitch holders, crochet hook size J/10 (6 mm).
Gauge: 18 sts and 24 rows = 4" (10 cm) in stockinette stitch (St st). Check your gauge before you begin.

special techniques
yarnover buttonhole
For a girl's sweater, work buttonholes 2 sts away from the center edge of right front as foll: On RS rows, k2, k2tog, yo, work to end of row; on WS rows, work to last 4 sts, yo, p2tog, p2.

For a boy's or unisex sweater, work buttonholes 2 sts away from the center edge of left front as foll: On RS rows, work to last 4 sts, k2tog, yo, k2; on WS rows, p2, yo, p2tog, work to end of row.

intarsia
The pawprint motifs in this sweater are knitted with separate lengths of yarn for each color block in intarsia technique (see page 106).

reading charts
If you need additional help reading the charts used for this pattern, see page 107.

back
With MC, loosely CO 51 (56, 61) sts. Work even in stockinette stitch (St st) for 5 (7, 7) rows, beg and ending with a WS (purl) row. Cont in St st, and work the pawprints border chart for your size. Row 1 (RS) is worked as foll: With MC k3 (4, 5); using separate strands of MC and CC yarn for each pawprint intarsia color area, work 4 reps of the 12 (13, 14)-st pattern repeat for Row 1. Cont in patt from chart as established until Row 10 has been completed. With MC, work even in St st until piece meas 5 (6, 7)" (12.5 [15, 18] cm) from CO, ending with a WS row. Shape for armholes: BO 2 sts at beg of next 2 rows—47 (52, 57) sts. For size 24 months *only*, work 6 more rows—piece meas 5 (6, 8)" (12.5 [15, 20.5] cm) from CO. Work Row 1

½" (1.3 cm) up from CO edge, then work 4 more buttonholes spaced approximately 1¼ (1¾, 2¼)" (3.2 [4.5, 5.5] cm) apart, with last buttonhole about ½" (1.3 cm) below beg of neck shaping. See the knitting tip about Intuitively Placed Buttonholes on page 101.

left front

With MC, loosely CO 27 (30, 33) sts. Work even in St st for 5 (7, 7) rows, beg and ending with a WS (purl) row. Cont in St st, and work the pawprints border chart for your size in intarsia technique as for back. Row 1 (RS) is worked as foll: With MC k3 (4, 5), work 2 reps of the 12 (13, 14)-st pattern repeat for Row 1. Cont in patt from chart as established until Row 10 has been completed. With MC, work even in St st until piece meas 5 (6, 7)"

(RS) of large pawprint chart as foll: With MC k14 (16, 19), work 19 sts from Row 1 of chart in intarsia, with MC k14 (17, 19). Cont in patt from chart as established until Row 22 has been completed. With MC, work even until piece meas 9¼ (11¼, 13¼)" (23.5 [28.5, 33.5] cm) from CO. Shape for back neck: Work across 13 (15, 16) sts, BO center 21 (22, 25) sts, work across rem 13 (15, 16) sts. Place rem sts for each shoulder on a separate st holder.

note about buttonholes

Using yarnover buttonhole method (see page 16), work 1st buttonhole

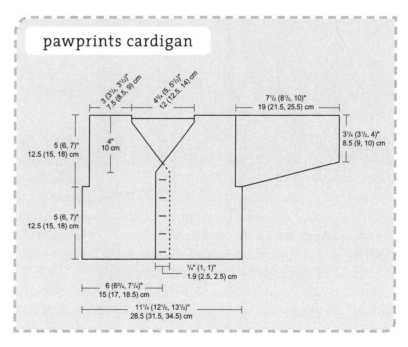

pawprints cardigan

3 (3¼, 3½)"
7.5 (8.5, 9) cm

4¾ (5, 5½)"
12 (12.5, 14) cm

7½ (8½, 10)"
19 (21.5, 25.5) cm

5 (6, 7)"
12.5 (15, 18) cm

4"
10 cm

3¼ (3½, 4)"
8.5 (9, 10) cm

5 (6, 7)"
12.5 (15, 18) cm

¾" (1, 1)"
1.9 (2.5, 2.5) cm

6 (6¾, 7¼)"
15 (17, 18.5) cm

11¼ (12½, 13½)"
28.5 (31.5, 34.5) cm

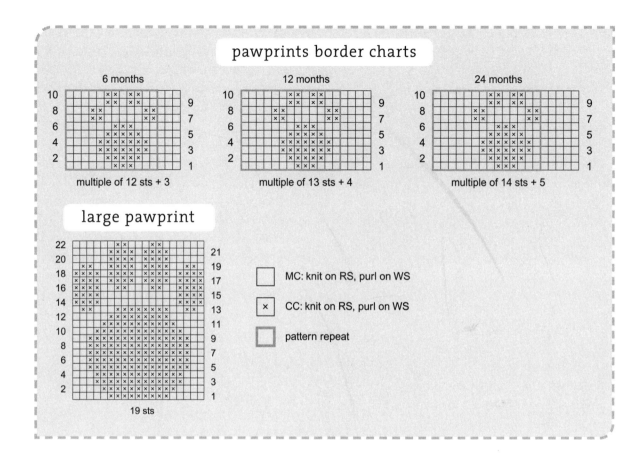

pawprints border charts

6 months

multiple of 12 sts + 3

12 months

multiple of 13 sts + 4

24 months

multiple of 14 sts + 5

large pawprint

19 sts

□ MC: knit on RS, purl on WS

☒ CC: knit on RS, purl on WS

□ pattern repeat

(12.5 [15, 18] cm) from CO, ending with a WS row. Shape for armhole: BO 2 sts at beg of next RS row, work to end—25 (28, 31) sts. Work even until piece meas 6 (8, 10)" (15 [20.5, 25.5] cm) from CO, ending with a WS row. Shape for neck: Beg with the next RS row, dec 1 st at neck edge (end of RS rows, beg of WS rows) every other row 7 (5, 3) times, then every row 5 (8, 12) times— 13 (15, 16) sts. Work even until front meas 10 (12, 14)" (25.5 [30.5, 35.5] cm) from CO, or same length as back. Place rem sts for shoulder on st holder.

right front

Work as for left front, reversing shaping by working armhole BO at the beg of a WS row, and working neck shaping at beg of RS rows or end of WS rows. When right front has been completed, place rem sts for shoulder on st holder.

join shoulders

Hold right front and back together with RS of fabric touching and WS of piece facing outward. Using three-needle bind-off technique (see page 108), join right shoulders. Join left shoulders in the same manner.

sleeves

With MC and RS facing, using crochet hook to assist if desired, pick up 45 (54, 63) sts evenly beg and ending at the armhole notches, including 1 st picked up from each armhole BO notch. Work in St st, dec to shape sleeve as foll: Dec 1 st each end of row every 4 rows 8 (11, 14) times—29 (32, 35) sts. Work even in St st, if necessary, until sleeve meas 7½ (8½, 10)" (19 [21.5, 25.5] cm) from pickup row, or desired length, ending with a WS row. Change to CC and knit 1 row on RS. Loosely BO all sts on WS on next row. Repeat for other sleeve.

finishing

Sew sleeve and side seams. Weave in all ends on WS. Front edging: With RS facing, CC and crochet hook, beg at the lower right front edge, pick up 108 (128, 148) sts evenly around front opening as foll: 26 (35, 44) sts along straight edge of right front, 18 sts along right V-neck shaping, 20 (22, 24) sts across back neck, 18 sts along left V-neck shaping, 26 (35, 44) sts along straight edge of left front. Loosely BO all sts on WS on next row. Lower edging: Hold sweater upside down with RS facing. With CC and RS facing, using crochet hook to assist if desired, beg at lower edge of left front, pick up 1 st for every st all along the lower edge. Loosely BO all sts on WS on next row. Weave in ends. Sew five buttons to opposite front to correspond with buttonholes. Please attach your buttons very securely to keep the baby from pulling them off and putting them in his or her mouth.

54/27/13'14

✱ this should have a better edging – garter st, or rib to prevent curling!

21st-century matinee set

(JACKET, BLANKET, LEGGINGS, ACCESSORIES)

this classic baby set makes a wonderful, retro-chic gift. Inspired by vintage pram sets, and updated here in chunky machine-washable wool, it's easy, it's fun and it's fast to knit. The set includes a snuggly V-neck jacket, easy-to-knit cozy leggings, a patchwork-style blanket and an accessories set with earflap hat, little socks, and thumbless mitts. The chunky gauge ensures you'll have time to knit all the pieces—but any combination or single piece will also make a fantastic and very functional baby gift.

Shown knit in baby blue for a boy, this can be easily adapted for a girl by choosing a soft color and moving the buttonholes on the jacket to the right front. Or make the whole set unisex by choosing bright or neutral colors, and placing the buttons on the left front as if for a boy.

The yarn requirements for each item in the set are given separately with the individual patterns. If you intend to make the entire set, you will need a total of approximately 1350 yards (1235 meters) of the main color, and 305 yards (280 meters) of the contrast color to make every piece in the largest size offered.

This set is presented in a very classic color scheme. To modernize its look, try garter stitch stripes of different colors. Either replace the neutral cream used here with a bolder color, or stripe the garter stitch ridges working two rows of each color before changing.

jacket

is the gender of the baby you're knitting for still a mystery? Make this jacket unisex by placing the buttonholes on the left front and choosing a bright or a neutral color scheme.

FINISHED SIZE
To fit 6 (12) months; shown in size 12 months.

FINISHED MEASUREMENTS
Chest circumference (buttoned): 20 (24)"; 51 (61) cm
Length from bottom edge to shoulder: 10 (12)"; 25.5 (30.5) cm
Sleeve length: 7½ (8½)"; 19 (21.5) cm

MATERIALS
Yarn: 210 (275) yards (195 [250] meters) bulky weight machine-washable wool that knits to correct gauge in main color (MC); 50 (55) yards (46 [50] meters) of contrasting color for garter stitch striped trim (CC).

Shown in Brown Sheep Company Lamb's Pride Superwash Bulky (100% machine-washable wool; 110 yards [100 meters]/100 grams), #SW71 misty blue (MC) and #SW10 alabaster (CC).

Needles: Size US 10½ (6.5 mm) straight needles, or size to obtain gauge.
Size US 9 (5.5 mm) straight needles for trim, or two sizes smaller than main needles. A 29" (70-cm) circular (circ) needle in this size is recommended for the button band.

Notions: Five ¾" (1.9-cm) buttons, measuring tape, yarn needle, scissors, four stitch holders, crochet hook size J/10 (6 mm).

Gauge: 13 sts and 17 rows = 4" (10 cm) in stockinette stitch (St st) using larger needles. Check your gauge before you begin.

special technique
yarnover buttonhole
Knit to the desired location of the buttonhole, k2tog, yo to form buttonhole. Follow directions for button band for placement.

note
The schematic shows the finished measurements of the jacket after sewing the pieces together. Because of the project's large gauge, the pieces are actually slightly wider than the measurements shown, so that the garment will be the correct size after one stitch at each side of the back, fronts, and sleeves has been used in the seams.

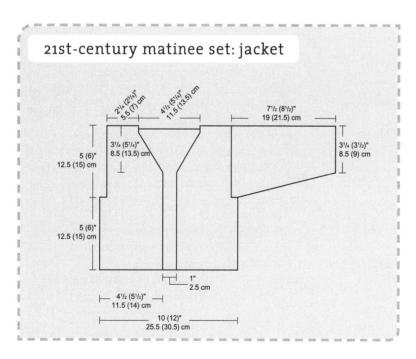

21st-century matinee set: jacket

back
With CC and smaller needles, CO 35 (41) sts. Work garter stitch stripes as foll: Knit 2 rows CC, knit 2 rows MC, knit 2 rows CC. Change to MC and larger needles. Work even in stockinette stitch (St st) until piece meas 5 (6)" (12.5 [15] cm) from CO, ending with a WS row. Shape for armholes: BO 2 sts at beg of next 2 rows—31 (37) sts. Work even until piece meas 9½ (11½)" (24 [29] cm) from CO. Shape for back neck: Work across 8 (10) sts, BO center 15 (17) sts, work across rem 8 (10) sts. Work even until piece meas 10 (12)" (25.5 [30.5] cm) from CO. Place rem sts for each shoulder on a separate st holder.

left front
With CC and smaller needles, CO 16 (19) sts. Work garter stitch stripes as foll: Knit 2 rows CC, knit 2 rows MC, knit 2 rows CC. Change to MC and larger needles. Work even in stockinette stitch (St st) until piece meas 5 (6)" (12.5 [15] cm) from CO, ending with a WS row. Shape for armhole: BO 2 sts at beg of next RS row, work to end—14 (17) sts. Work even until piece meas 6¾" (17 cm) from CO, ending with a WS row. Shape for neck: Beg with the next RS row, dec 1 st at neck edge (end of RS rows, beg of WS rows) every 3 rows 0 (6) times, then every other row 6 (1) time(s)—8 (10) sts.

Work even until front meas 10 (12)" (25.5 [30.5] cm) from CO, or same length as back. Place rem sts for shoulder on st holder.

right front

Work as for left front, reversing shaping by working armhole BO at the beg of a WS row, and working neck shaping at beg of RS rows or end of WS rows. When right front has been completed, place rem sts for shoulder on st holder.

join shoulders

Hold right front and back together with RS of fabric touching and WS of piece facing outward. Using three-needle bind-off technique (see page 108), join right shoulders. Join left shoulders in the same manner.

sleeves

With MC, larger needles, and RS facing, using crochet hook to assist if desired, pick up 35 (41) sts evenly beg and ending at the armhole notches, including 1 st picked up from each armhole BO notch. Work in St st, dec to shape sleeve as foll: Dec 1 st each end of row every 4 rows 6 times, then every 2 rows 0 (2) times—23 (25) sts. Work even in St st until sleeve meas 6½ (7½)" (16.5 [19] cm) from pickup row, or 1" (2.5 cm) less than desired length, ending with a WS row. Change to CC and smaller needles. Knit 2 rows CC, knit 2 rows MC, knit 2 rows CC. Loosely BO all sts on WS on next row using CC. Repeat for other sleeve.

finishing

note about buttonholes

Place yarnover buttonholes on the right front button band for a girl's sweater, or left front band for boy's or unisex sweater (see page 21). Work 1st buttonhole ½" (1.3 cm) up from CO edge, then work 4 more buttonholes spaced slightly less than 1½" (3.8 cm) apart, with last buttonhole ½" (1.3 cm) below beg of neck shaping. The buttonholes will be about 2 sts in from the CO and beg of neck shaping, and have about 2 sts between them. You can also "eyeball" the placement; see the knitting tip about Intuitively Placed Buttonholes on page 101.

button band

With CC, smaller needle, and RS facing, using crochet hook to assist if desired, beg at the lower right front edge, pick up 84 (92) sts evenly around front opening as foll: 22 sts along straight edge of right front, 13 (16) sts along right V-neck shaping, 14 (16) sts across back neck, 13 (16) sts along left V-neck shaping, 22 sts along straight edge of left front. Knit 1 row on WS. Change to MC and knit 1 row, making 5 yarnover buttonholes as given in note above. Knit 1 more row with MC. Change to CC and knit 1 row. BO all sts loosely on next row with CC. Sew sleeve and side seams. Weave in ends. Sew five buttons to opposite front to correspond with buttonholes. Please attach your buttons very securely to keep the baby from pulling them off and putting them in his or her mouth.

blanket

this patchwork-style blanket in stockinette and garter stitch stripes is knit in five easy strips that are sewn together at the end, which makes for a portable project. The bulky yarn makes it knit up fast, and the machine-washable wool makes it practical—perfect for both knitting and giving. To make this project gender neutral (or to make it "girly") play with different color combinations.

FINISHED SIZE
Approximately 29" (73.5 cm) square.

MATERIALS
Yarn: 500 yards (460 meters) bulky weight machine-washable wool that knits to correct gauge in main color (MC); 200 yards (185 meters) of contrasting color for garter stitch stripes (CC).

Shown in Brown Sheep Company Lamb's Pride Superwash Bulky (100% machine-washable wool; 110 yards [100 meters]/100 grams), #SW71 misty blue (MC) and #SW10 alabaster (CC).

Needles: Size US 10½ (6.5 mm) straight needles, or size to obtain gauge.

Notions: Measuring tape, yarn needle, scissors, crochet hook size J/10 (6 mm).

Gauge: 13 sts and 17 rows = 4" (10 cm) in stockinette stitch (St st). Check your gauge before you begin.

note

Each strip is one block wide and five blocks high. Before sewing up, each block measures about 6" (15 cm) wide and 5¾" (14.5 cm) high. The blocks will be about 5¾" (14.5 cm) square after assembling.

strip one (make 3)

*With MC, CO 20 sts and work in stockinette stitch (St st) for 24 rows, ending with a WS row—first block completed. Join CC and [knit 2 rows CC, knit 2 rows MC] 7 times, then knit 2 more rows CC (30 rows and 15 stripes total)—second block completed. Rep from * one more time—4 blocks completed. Change to MC and work 24 rows in St st—5 blocks completed. Loosely BO all sts. Make two more strips exactly the same way.

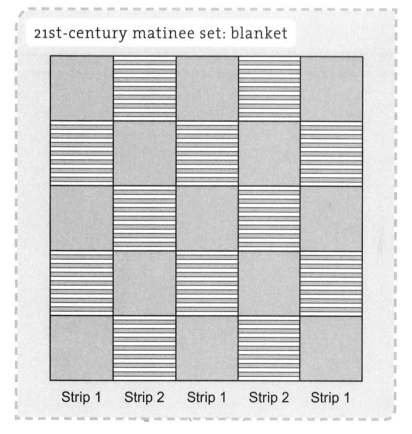

21st-century matinee set: blanket

Strip 1   Strip 2   Strip 1   Strip 2   Strip 1

strip two (make 2)

*With CC, CO 20 sts. [Knit 2 rows CC, knit 2 rows MC] 7 times, then knit 2 more rows CC (30 rows and 15 stripes total)—first block completed. Change to MC and work in St st for 24 rows, ending with a WS row—second block completed. Rep from * one more time—4 blocks completed. Join CC and work the first block (garter stripes) one more time—5 blocks completed. Loosely BO all sts. Make another strip exactly the same way.

finishing

Arrange strips side-by-side as shown in diagram. Invisibly sew the strips together, lining up where the blocks change, checkerboard fashion, and carefully matching the corners of the blocks. With RS facing, crochet hook and MC, work 1 row of single crochet around the entire edge. Weave in ends on WS.

leggings

these warm and easy-care leggings are worked in two pieces, each consisting of one leg and half of the "waist" area. Make two, and then sew them together at the center front and back, and around the inseam. This is a really fast, easy-to-knit project parents will love—the high waist keeps a diapered bottom covered, even when said bottom is crawling!

FINISHED SIZE
To fit 6–9 (12) months; shown in size 6–9 months.

FINISHED MEASUREMENTS
Hip circumference: 23 (25)"; 58.5 (63.5) cm
Crotch height to lower edge of waistband: 7 (8)"; 18 (20.5) cm
Waistband height: 3½" (9 cm) for both sizes
Leg length: 9 (12)"; 23 (30.5) cm

MATERIALS
Yarn: 245 (320) yards (225 [290] meters) bulky weight machine-washable wool that knits to correct gauge.

Shown in Brown Sheep Company Lamb's Pride Superwash Bulky (100% machine-washable wool; 110 yards [100 meters]/100 grams), #SW71 misty blue.
Needles: Size US 10½ (6.5 mm) straight needles, or size to obtain gauge.
Size US 9 (5.5 mm) straight needles for ribbing, or two sizes smaller than main needles.
Notions: Measuring tape, yarn needle, scissors, scraps of waste yarn.
Gauge: 13 sts and 17 rows = 4" (10 cm) in stockinette stitch (St st) using larger needles. Check your gauge before you begin.

note

The schematic shows the finished measurements of the leggings, after sewing the pieces together. Because of the project's large gauge, the pieces are actually slightly wider than the measurements shown, so that the garment will be the correct size after one stitch at each side of each piece has been used in the seams.

leggings (make 2 identical pieces)

With smaller needles CO 30 (33) sts. Work in k1, p1 ribbing for 3" (7.5 cm) or desired length of cuff, ending with a WS row, and inc 4 sts evenly in last row of ribbing—34 (37) sts. Change to larger needles. Work even in stockinette stitch (St st) until piece meas 5¼ (8¼)" (13.5 [21] cm) from top of ribbing, or ¾" (1.9 cm) less than desired leg length, ending with a WS row. Increase for crotch: Inc 1 st at each end of row for the next 3 rows—40 (43) sts; piece meas about 9 (12)" (23 [30.5] cm) from CO. With scrap yarn, mark both ends of the last row for seam placement. Cont in St st, work even until piece meas 7 (8)" (18 [20.5] cm) above markers, ending with a WS row, and dec 4 sts evenly in last row—36 (39) sts. Change to smaller needles. Work in k1, p1 ribbing for 3½" (9 cm), or desired height of waistband. BO all sts loosely. Repeat for other legging piece.

finishing

Sew the pieces together at each side, from the markers above the crotch shaping to the lower edge of the waist ribbing. Sew the waistband seams, and if you would like to be able to fold the waistband to the outside, reverse the seams so that the right side of the seam allowances will show when waistband is folded down. Refold the pieces so that the seams just completed are at the center front and back. Sew the inseam from the CO edge of one cuff, up the leg to the crotch markers, and down the other leg to the end of the cuff, as shown in schematic. Weave in all ends on WS.

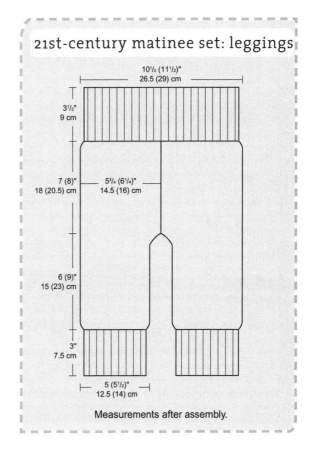

21st-century matinee set: leggings

10½ (11½)"
26.5 (29) cm

3½"
9 cm

7 (8)"
18 (20.5) cm

5¾ (6¼)"
14.5 (16) cm

6 (9)"
15 (23) cm

3"
7.5 cm

5 (5½)"
12.5 (14) cm

Measurements after assembly.

accessories (hat, sockies, and thumbless mitts)

here are little gifts that earn big "oohs" and "aahs" at baby showers. These tiny accessories make great projects for knitters who want to become comfortable knitting in the round using double-pointed needles. The sockies are knit using an "afterthought heel." Each sock is knit as a tube with some stitches temporarily knit with scrap yarn for minimal interruption. Later, these stitches are knit out from the tube to make a heel fashioned the same as the toe. If you are feeling adventuresome, try it. You will improve your knitting repertoire, and keep a lot of little feet warm.

hat

FINISHED SIZE
To fit 6 (12, 24) months; shown in size 12 months.

FINISHED MEASUREMENTS
Circumference: 14¾ (15½, 18)"; 37.5 (39.5, 45.5) cm

MATERIALS
Yarn: 85 (90, 100) yards (78 [82, 90] meters) bulky
weight machine-washable wool that knits to
correct gauge in main color (MC); 13 (14, 15) yards
(12 [13, 14] meters) of contrasting color for garter
stitch stripes (CC).

Shown in Brown Sheep Company Lamb's Pride
Superwash Bulky (100% machine-washable wool; 110
yards [100 meters]/100 grams), #SW71 misty blue
(MC) and #SW10 alabaster (CC).
Needles: Size US 10½ (6.5 mm) set of four double-pointed
needles (dpn) or size to obtain gauge.
Notions: Measuring tape, yarn needle, scissors, two
stitch holders, stitch marker.
Gauge: 13 sts and 17 rows = 4" (10 cm) in stockinette stitch
(St st) in the round (rnd). Check your gauge before
you begin.

note

To work garter stitch stripes in the round, you must alternate knit and purl rounds as foll:

Stripe 1: With MC, knit 1 rnd, purl 1 rnd.

Stripe 2: With CC, knit 1 rnd, purl 1 rnd—4 rnds and 2 garter stitch stripes completed.

Rep these 4 rnds as required for patt.

earflaps (make 2)

With CC, CO 3 sts. Working back and forth in garter stitch (knit every row), knit 2 rows CC, then knit 2 rows MC for garter stitch stripes. *At the same time,* shape earflaps as foll: Beg with the first RS row, inc 1 st at each end of needle every 4 rows (every other RS row) 3 times, ending with a MC stripe—9 sts; 12 rows and 6 garter stitch stripes completed. Knit 2 more rows with CC—7 stripes completed, earflap meas about 2½" (6.5 cm) from CO. Place sts on holder. Work second earflap the same as the first.

base of hat

In this step you will CO sts for the base of the hat at the same time as you knit across the tops of the earflaps to join them to the bottom edge of the hat. Using MC and dpn or circ needle, hold first earflap with RS facing and knit across 9 sts. Using the knitting-on method (see page 102), CO 15 (16, 20) sts. Hold second earflap with RS facing and knit across 9 sts. Using the knitting-on method, CO (15, 16, 20) sts—48 (50, 58) sts. Place a marker to indicate the beg of the rnd. Purl 1 rnd with MC.

hat

Cont in garter stitch stripes for 6 more rnds, working 2 rnds CC, 2 rnds MC, and 2 rnds CC. Change to MC and work in St st in the rnd (knit all sts every rnd) until hat meas 3½ (4, 4½)" (9 [10, 11.5] cm) from sts CO for base of hat.

crown

Shape crown of hat as foll:

Rnd 1: K4 (0, 4), *k8, k2tog; rep from * to last 4 (0, 4) sts, end k4 (0, 4)—44 (45, 53) sts.
Rnd 2: Knit 1 rnd even.
Rnd 3: K4 (0, 4), *k7, k2tog; rep from * to last 4 (0, 4) sts, end k4 (0, 4)—40 (40, 48) sts.
Rnd 4: Knit 1 rnd even.
Rnd 5: *K6, k2tog; rep from * to end—35 (35, 42) sts.
Rnd 6: Knit 1 rnd even.
Rnd 7: *K5, k2tog; rep from * to end—30 (30, 36) sts.
Rnd 8: Knit 1 rnd even.

For largest size *only*, work 1 rnd as foll: *K4, k2tog; rep from * to end; then work 1 rnd even—30 sts rem for all sizes.

On the next rnd, work k2tog all the way around—15 sts. Work 1 rnd even. On the next rnd, work as foll: K2tog 7 times, k1—8 sts.

top knot

Work rem 8 sts in the rnd until the extension meas about 5" (12.5 cm) from last k2tog rnd. CO all sts. Weave in end to WS of hat. Tie the extension in an overhand knot, as shown in photograph.

ties (make 2)

Cut six strands of MC, each 64" (162.5 cm) long. Thread three strands on yarn needle and pass the needle through the lower CO point of one earflap. Pull the ends of the strands even so their halfway point is at the earflap, and you have six 32" (81.5-cm) lengths hanging down from the flap to work with. Remove the needle. Braid the ends, using two strands for each element of the braid, until about 4" (10 cm) of the strands rem, or desired length. Tie the ends in an overhand knot and trim them even. Repeat for other tie. Weave in all ends on WS.

FINISHED SIZE
To fit 6 (9–12) months; shown in size 9–12 months.

FINISHED MEASUREMENTS
Circumference: 4¾ (5¼)"; 12 (13.5) cm
Leg length: 2½ (3)"; 6.5 (7.5) cm
Foot length: 3¾ (5)"; 9.5 (12.5) cm

MATERIALS
Yarn: 80 (110) yards (73 [100] meters) bulky weight machine-washable wool that knits to correct gauge in main color (MC); 18 (20) yards (17 [18] meters) of contrasting color for garter stitch stripes, heels, and toes (CC).

Shown in Brown Sheep Company Lamb's Pride Superwash Bulky (100% machine-washable wool; 110 yards [100 meters]/100 grams), #SW71 misty blue (MC) and #SW10 alabaster (CC).
Needles: Size US 10 (6 mm) set of four double-pointed needles (dpn), or size to obtain gauge.
Notions: Measuring tape, yarn needle, scissors, stitch marker, 2 yards (2 meters) of a smooth, contrasting scrap yarn.
Gauge: 15 sts and 20 rows = 4" (10 cm) in stockinette stitch (St st) in the round (rnd). Check your gauge before you begin.

note

To customize the sockies, measure the sole of baby's foot by tracing around it on a piece of paper. Note length from the end of the big toe to the base of the heel. Take this length and subtract about 3" (7.5 cm). This is the length to knit between the waste yarn stitches for heel placement and the beginning of the toe. The toe and afterthought heel will each add about 1½" (3.8 cm) to the total length of the foot.

cuff

With CC, loosely CO 18 (20) sts. Join for working in the rnd, being careful not to twist, and place marker to indicate beg of rnd. Purl 1 rnd. Change to MC and knit 1 rnd, purl 1 rnd. Change to CC and knit 1 rnd, purl 1 rnd—6 rnds and 3 garter stitch stripes completed. Change to MC and work in St st in the rnd (knit all sts every rnd) until piece meas 2½ (3)" (6.5 [7.5] cm) from CO.

heel placement

With MC, k9 (10) sts. Cut MC, and with contrasting scrap yarn knit across rem 9 (10) sts to end.

foot

Rejoin MC and work even in St st on all sts until foot measures ¾ (2)" (1.9 [5] cm) from scrap yarn, or desired length.

toe

Rearrange sts on 2 needles (ndls), 9 (10) sts on each ndl. The sts on one of the ndls should exactly correspond to the scrap yarn sts for heel placement so that your toe and heel will line up properly. Cut MC, leaving a 6-to-8" (15-to-20.5-cm) tail. Join CC. Working in the rnd with 3 ndls, knit 1 rnd even. Beg toe shaping as foll:

Rnd 1: *K1, ssk, knit to last 3 sts on ndl, k2tog, k1; rep from * for second ndl—14 (16) sts.

Rnd 2: Knit 1 rnd even.

Rep the last 2 rnds 3 more times—2 (4) sts rem. Cut CC, leaving a 12" (30.5-cm) tail. Thread scrap yarn on yarn needle and run through all sts to hold them. Turn sockie inside out and return sts to 2 ndls. With wrong side of sockie facing you, use CC tail and three-needle bind-off technique (see page 108) to join toe sts. Secure tail, and weave in end on WS.

heel

Carefully remove the scrap yarn and place live sts on 2 ndls as they become available, 9 (10) sts on each ndl. Join CC and knit 1 rnd, picking up 1 st in 2 corners between the ndls—20 (22) sts, 10 (11) sts on each ndl. Knit 3 rnds.

Rnd 1: *K1, ssk, knit to last 3 sts on ndl, k2tog, k1; rep from * for second ndl—16 (18) sts.

Rnd 2: Knit 1 rnd even.

Rep the last 2 rnds once more—12 (14) sts, 6 (7) sts on each ndl. Cut CC, leaving a 12" (30.5-cm) tail. Thread scrap yarn on yarn needle and run through all sts to hold them. Turn sockie inside out and return sts to 2 ndls. With wrong side of sockie facing you, use CC tail and three-needle bind-off technique (see page 108) to join heel sts. Secure tail, and weave in end on WS.

finishing

Weave in any rem ends to WS. While weaving in ends, use the tails to close up any small holes at the sides of the heel. Work second sockie the same as the first.

FINISHED SIZE
To fit up to 24 months.

FINISHED MEASUREMENTS
Circumference: 6" (15 cm)
Length: 5" (12.5 cm)

MATERIALS
Yarn: 45 yards (40 meters) bulky weight machine-washable wool that knits to correct gauge in main color (MC); 15 yards (15 meters) of contrasting color for garter stitch striped cuffs (CC).

Shown in Brown Sheep Company Lamb's Pride Superwash Bulky (100% machine-washable wool; 110 yards [100 meters]/100 grams), #SW71 misty blue (MC) and #SW10 alabaster (CC).
Needles: Size US 10 (6 mm) set of four double-pointed needles (dpn), or size to obtain gauge.
Notions: Measuring tape, yarn needle, scissors, stitch marker.
Gauge: 15 sts and 20 rows = 4" (10 cm) in stockinette stitch (St st) in the round (rnd). Check your gauge before you begin.

mitts

With CC, loosely CO 22 sts. Join for working in the rnd, being careful not to twist, and place marker to indicate beg of rnd. Purl 1 rnd. Change to MC and knit 1 rnd, purl 1 rnd. Change to CC and knit 1 rnd, purl 1 rnd—6 rnds and 3 garter stitch stripes completed. Change to MC and work in St st in the rnd (knit all sts every rnd) for 3 rnds. Work an eyelet rnd for drawstring as foll: *Yo, k2tog; rep from * to end. Cont in St st until piece meas 4½" (11.5 cm) from CO edge.

Dec Rnd 1: *K2, k2tog; rep from * to last 2 sts, end k2—17 sts.
Dec Rnd 2: *K2tog twice, *K1, k2tog; rep from * to last 4 sts, end k2tog twice—10 sts.
Dec Rnd 3: K2tog around—5 sts.

Cut yarn, leaving a 12" (30.5-cm) tail. Thread tail on yarn needle and draw through all sts. Pull yarn tight to close top of mitt. Secure tail, and weave in end on WS.

finishing

Weave in any rem ends to WS. Work second mitt the same as the first.

ties (make 2)

Cut six strands of MC, each 54" (137 cm) long. Using a bundle of three strands, tie an overhand knot about 2" (5 cm) from the end. Braid the strands for 16" (40.5 cm), or until about 3" (7.5 cm) of the strands rem, or desired length. Tie the ends in an overhand knot and trim the tails at each end of the tie to 1" (2.5 cm). Repeat for other tie. Beg at the center back of each mitt, thread the ties through the eyelet holes, pull the ends even, and tie in a bow.

infant gift set

(SWEATER, RECEIVING CLOTH, HAT)

the perfect shower gift, this adorable baby set includes a simple sweater knit in reverse stockinette stitch with a single cable accent, and a coordinating receiving cloth and hat. Any combination of one or all of the pieces make a perfect, practical baby gift. The hat and cloth are nice beginner knitter's projects, and the small sweater is a great introduction to knitting a garment. Shown here in a delightfully soft and easy-care textured cotton yarn in unbleached undyed natural, it is just warm enough for layering and so gentle on a baby's delicate skin. Make the sweater with the buttons on the "boy's" side for a unisex gift.

This set is an easy way to try your hand at knitting cables, which are a fun and easy way to make a simple sweater look stunning and impressive! You can find helpful information about working cables and reading a knitting chart in the "Knitting Tips" section.

sweater

FINISHED SIZE
To fit 6 (12, 24) months; shown in size 6 months.

FINISHED MEASUREMENTS
Chest circumference (buttoned): 20 (25, 30)", 51 (63.5, 76) cm
Length from bottom edge to shoulder: 10 (12, 14)", 25.5 (30.5, 35.5) cm
Sleeve length: 7½ (8½, 10)"; 19 (21.5, 25.5) cm

MATERIALS
Yarn: 250 (400, 555) yards (230 [365, 510] meters) Aran weight cotton that knits to correct gauge.

Shown in Mission Falls 1824 Cotton (100% cotton; 84 yards [77 meters]/50 grams), #102 ivory.
Needles: Size US 8 (5 mm) straight needles, or size to obtain gauge.
Notions: Five ½" (1.3-cm) buttons, cable needle, measuring tape, yarn needle, scissors, four stitch holders, crochet hook size J/10 (6 mm).
Gauge: 18 sts and 24 rows = 4" (10 cm) in reverse stockinette stitch (rev St st); each 4-st cable meas ¾" (1.9 cm) wide. Check your gauge before you begin.

special technique

yarnover buttonhole

For a girl's sweater, work buttonholes 2 sts away from the center edge of right front as foll: On RS rows, p2, p2tog, yo, work to end of row; on WS rows, work to last 4 sts, yo, k2tog, k2.

For a boy's or unisex sweater, work buttonholes 2 sts away from the center edge of left front as foll: On RS rows, work to last 4 sts, p2tog, yo, p2; on WS rows, k2, yo, k2tog, work to end of row.

reading charts

If you need additional help reading the charts used for this pattern, see page 107.

back

Loosely CO 45 (56, 67) sts. Work even in rev stockinette stitch (rev St st: purl all sts on RS, knit all sts on WS) until piece meas 5 (6, 7)" (12.5 [15, 18] cm) from CO, ending with a WS row. Shape for armholes: BO 2 sts at beg of next 2 rows—41 (52, 63) sts. Work even until piece meas 9½ (11½, 13½)" (24 [29, 34.5] cm) from CO. Shape for back neck: Work across 9 (14, 18) sts, BO center 23 (24, 27) sts, join second ball of yarn and work across rem 9 (14, 18) sts. Working both sides separately, cont in rev St st until piece meas 10 (12, 14)" (25.5 [30.5, 35.5] cm) from beg. Place rem sts for each shoulder on a separate st holder.

note about buttonholes

Using yarnover buttonhole method (see above), work 1st buttonhole ½" (1.3 cm) up from CO edge, then work 4 more buttonholes spaced approximately 1⅝ (2⅛, 2⅝)" (4.5 [5.5, 6.5] cm) apart, with last buttonhole about ½" (1.3 cm) below beg of neck shaping. See the knitting tip about Intuitively Placed Buttonholes on page 101.

left front

Loosely CO 25 (31, 37) sts. Work setup row as foll: (WS) K5, p4 for cable, k16 (22, 28). Beg with the next row, work patts as foll: (RS) Work 16 (22, 28) sts rev St st, work 4 sts according to Row 1 of right cable chart (see charts on page 42), work 5 sts rev St st. Cont in patts as established, repeating Rows 1–4 of right cable chart, until piece meas 5 (6, 7)" (12.5 [15, 18] cm) from CO, ending with a WS row. Shape for armhole: BO 2 sts at beg of next RS row, work to end—23 (29, 35) sts. Work even until piece meas 7½ (9½, 11½)" (19 [24, 29] cm) from CO, ending with a RS row. Shape for front neck: (WS) BO 7 (8, 10) sts, work to end—16 (21, 25) sts. Dec 1 st at neck edge every row 7 times—9 (14, 18) sts. Cont in rev St st until piece meas 10 (12, 14)" (25.5 [30.5, 35.5] cm) from beg. Place rem sts for shoulder on st holder.

right front

Loosely CO 25 (31, 37) sts. Work setup row as foll: (WS) K16 (22, 28), p4 for cable, k5. Beg with the next row, work patts as foll: (RS) Work 5 sts rev St st, work 4 sts according to Row 1 of left cable chart (see page 42), work 16 (22, 28) sts rev St st. Cont in patts as established, repeating Rows 1–4 of left cable chart, until piece meas 5 (6, 7)" (12.5 [15, 18] cm) from CO, ending with a RS row. Cont as for left front, reversing shaping by working armhole BO at the beg of a WS row, and working neck shaping at beg of RS rows or end of WS rows. When right front has been completed, place rem sts for shoulder on st holder.

join shoulders

Hold right front and back together with RS of fabric touching and WS of piece facing outward. Using three-needle bind-off technique (see page 108), join right shoulders. Join left shoulders in the same manner.

sleeves

With RS facing, using crochet hook to assist if desired, pick up 45 (54, 63) sts evenly beg and ending at the armhole notches, including 1 st picked up from each armhole BO notch. Work in rev St st, dec to shape sleeve as foll: Dec 1 st each end of row every 4 rows 9 (11, 14) times—27 (32, 35) sts. Work even in rev St st, if necessary, until sleeve meas 7½ (8½, 10)" (19 [21.5, 25.5] cm) from pickup row, or desired length. BO all sts loosely. Repeat for other sleeve.

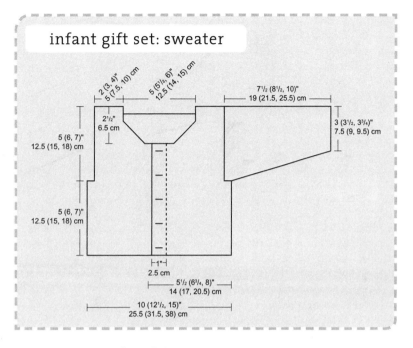

infant gift set: sweater

finishing

Sew sleeve and side seams. Weave in all ends on WS. Crochet edge: With RS facing, crochet hook, beg at a side seam, work a row of reverse single crochet (sometimes called crab stitch, creates a scalloped effect) around the bottom, front and neck edges, ending back where you started. Fasten off last st and weave in ends. Work a row of reverse single crochet in the same manner around sleeve cuffs. Sew five buttons to opposite front to correspond with buttonholes. Please attach your buttons very securely to keep the baby from pulling them off and putting them in his or her mouth.

receiving cloth

FINISHED SIZE
Approximately 8¼" (21 cm) wide and 18½" (47 cm) long, not including crochet edging.

MATERIALS
Yarn: 150 yards (137 meters) Aran weight cotton that knits to correct gauge.
Shown in Mission Falls 1824 Cotton (100% cotton; 84 yards [77 meters]/50 grams), #102 ivory.

Needles: Size US 8 (5 mm) straight needles, or size to obtain gauge.
Notions: Cable needle, measuring tape, yarn needle, scissors, crochet hook size J/10 (6 mm).
Gauge: 18 sts and 24 rows = 4" (10 cm) in reverse stockinette stitch (rev St st); each 4-st cable meas ¾" (1.9 cm) wide. Check your gauge before you begin.

special technique

reading charts

If you need additional help reading the charts used for this pattern, see page 107.

cloth

Loosely CO 38 sts. Work setup row as foll: (WS) K4, p4 for cable, k22, p4 for cable, k4. Beg with the next row, work patts as foll: (RS) Work 4 sts rev St st (see page 42), work 4 sts according to Row 1 of right cable chart, work 22 sts rev St st, work 4 sts according to Row 1 of left cable chart (see page 42), work 4 sts rev St st. Cont in patts as established, repeating Rows 1–4 of cable charts, until piece meas about 18½" (47 cm) from CO, and ending with Row 1 of patts (cable crossing row). BO all sts loosely.

finishing

Crochet edge: With RS facing, using crochet hook, beg at one corner, work a row of reverse single crochet (sometimes called crab stitch, creates a scalloped effect) around all four sides of cloth, working 3 sts into each corner to turn, and ending back where you started. Fasten off last st. Weave in all ends on WS.

hat

FINISHED SIZE
To fit 6–12 (24) months; shown in size 6–12 months.

FINISHED MEASUREMENTS
Circumference: 16 (18), 40.5 (45.5) cm

MATERIALS
Yarn: 70 (80) yards (64 [73] meters) Aran weight cotton
that knits to correct gauge.
Shown in Mission Falls 1824 Cotton (100% cotton; 84
yards [77 meters]/50 grams), #102 ivory.

Needles: Size US 8 (5 mm) set of four double-pointed
needles (dpn), or size to obtain gauge. A 16 " (40-cm)
circular needle (circ) may also be used for the
beginning of the hat, changing to dpn when there
are too few stitches to continue on the circ.
Notions: Measuring tape, yarn needle, scissors, stitch
marker.
Gauge: 18 sts and 24 rows = 4" (10 cm) in reverse
stockinette stitch (rev St st). Check your gauge before
you begin.

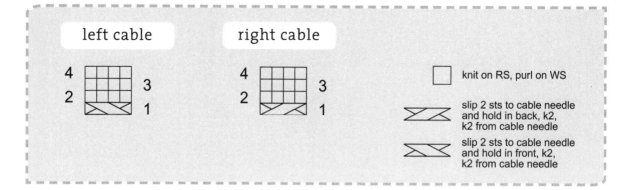

hat

With dpn or circ needle, loosely CO 72 (81) sts. Join, for working in the round (rnd), being careful not to twist, and place marker to indicate beg of rnd. Work in stockinette stitch (St st: knit all sts every rnd) until piece meas 1" (2.5 cm) from CO. Change to reverse stockinette stitch (rev St st: purl all sts every rnd) and work even until hat meas 4¾ (5¼)" (12 [13.5] cm) from CO with bottom rolled edge flattened out. Note: If you would prefer not to purl every rnd, you can flip the hat inside out and knit every rnd instead.

crown

If you are working the hat inside out, substitute knits for purls in the foll directions. Otherwise, cont to purl all sts on RS. Decrease as follows:

Rnd 1: *P4, p2tog, rep from * to last 0 (3) sts, end p0 (3)—60 (68) sts.

Rnd 2: *P3, p2tog; rep from * to last 0 (3) sts, end p0 (3)—48 (55) sts.

Rnd 3: *P2, p2tog; rep from * to last 0 (3) sts, end p0 (3)—36 (42) sts.

Rnd 4: *P1, p2tog; rep from * to end—24 (28) sts.

Rnd 5: P2tog to end—12 (14) sts.

Rnd 6: Purl 1 rnd even.

Rnd 7: Rep Rnd 5—6 (7) sts.

Cut yarn, leaving a 12" (30.5-cm) tail. Thread tail on yarn needle and draw through all sts. Pull yarn tight to close top of hat. Secure tail. Weave in ends on WS. Allow St st border at bottom edge to roll up.

toy dog for everyone

KNITTED DOG WITH JACKET

this easy little cutie is modeled after a design originally intended for children to knit. Get creative and try different colors, add stripes or add spots. Make the ears longer or different colors. Give your dog a bobtail or a long curly one. Make a fatter dog by incorporating more stitches at the center, or remove stitches for a skinny one. If you're making this toy as a gift, match the recipient's breed with colors that resemble their dog's fur. When making for a baby, consider using pure wool as stuffing to create a nice, all-natural toy. When making for a dog, stuff with wool, fiberfill, or cedar chips (available at pet or natural-food stores). If using cedar chips, consider tightening up the stitch gauge to prevent the stuffing from leaking out.

FINISHED MEASUREMENTS

Dog length from nose to tip of tail: about 10" (25.5 cm)

Dog height from bottom of feet to top of back: about 4½" (11.5 cm)

Finished jacket length from collar to base of tail: about 5½" (14 (cm)

MATERIALS

Yarn: 80 yards (72 meters) of any yarn that knits to between 3½ and 4½ stitches per inch in main color for body (MC); 45 yards (41 meters) of same yarn in contrasting color for jacket (CC, optional); small amounts of accent colors for nose, eyes, tongue, and tip of tail.

Shown in Mission Falls 1824 Wool (100% machine-washable Merino wool; 85 yards [78 meters]/50 grams), #007 cocoa (MC), #011 poppy (CC), with #008 earth (dark brown), #026 zinnia (pink), and #005 raven (black) for tip of tail and muzzle, tongue, and eyes.

Needles: Size US 8 (5 mm) straight needles for dog, or size to obtain gauge.

Size US 7 (4.5 mm) straight needles for jacket (optional).

Notions: Measuring tape, yarn needle, scissors, crochet hook size H/8 (5 mm), wool fiber or polyester fiberfill for stuffing, two ½" (1.3-cm) buttons for jacket (optional).

Gauge: 3½ to 4½ sts = 1" (2.5 cm) in stockinette stitch (St st). Exact gauge is not critical for this project, as long as you produce a fabric tight enough to contain your chosen stuffing. For the dog shown, 18 sts and 22 rows = 4" (10 cm) in St st using larger needles.

toy dog

tail

With MC or color for tip of tail, loosely CO 10 sts. Work even in St st for 5 rows if using an accent color for tail. Change to MC, or cont in MC until piece meas 2½" (6.5 cm) from CO.

back legs

At the beg of the next 2 rows, CO 18 sts for back legs—46 sts. Work even in St st until back legs meas 1½ to 2" (3.8 to 5 cm) from CO, ending with a WS row. At the beg of the next 2 rows, BO 7 sts—32 sts.

midsection

Work even for 3" (7.5 cm), or desired length for midsection, ending with a WS row.

front legs

At the beg of the next 2 rows, CO 7 sts for front legs—46 sts. Work even until front legs meas 1½" to 2" (3.8 to 5 cm) from CO, ending with a WS row. At the beg of the next 2 rows, BO 11 sts—24 sts.

neck and head

Work even on 24 sts for neck and head until piece meas 1" (2.5 cm) above last BO row, or desired length for neck and head, ending with a WS row. Change to accent color for muzzle if you are using one. Otherwise, cont with MC and shape muzzle as foll: Dec 1 st at each side every other row twice—20 sts. On the next RS row, work k2tog to end—10 sts. Cut yarn, leaving a 20" (51-cm) tail. Thread tail on yarn needle and draw through all sts. Pull yarn tight to close end of muzzle. Secure end, and weave in on WS.

assembly and stuffing

Sew the legs into tubes, matching the dotted lines of the seams as shown on diagram, working from the body toward the feet, and then gather the bottom of each foot closed. For example, for the left back leg, match the edges indicated by the dashed line, and sew them together working toward the foot. Run the sewing strand through the selvedge sts at the bottom of the leg, and gather them tightly closed, like a drawstring, to close the foot. When the legs have been completed, sew the tail and head into tubes in the same manner, matching the dotted lines as shown on diagram, and gathering the ends closed. Weave in ends on WS. Using the stopper end of a knitting needle or the eraser end of a pencil, stuff the legs, head, and tail firmly. Sew the back legs together underneath the tail, and sew the front legs together underneath the head. Stuff the body through the opening in the midsection, and then sew the seam closed. Curl the end of the tail up as shown, if desired, and secure the curl of the tail with a few sts. Weave in ends.

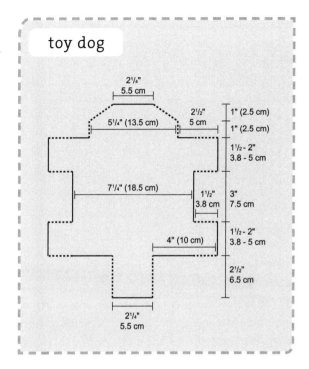

toy dog

ears

Choose the perfect spot for the ears. With MC and using crochet hook to assist, if desired, pick up 5 sts at the perfect location. Work 2 rows St st with the purl side facing the end of the nose. On the next 2 rows, dec 1 st at each end—1 st. Cut yarn and draw through last st to secure. Weave in ends. Rep for other ear. For better definition at the top of the head, pinch the head fabric at the base of each ear, and sew a small st or two through both pinched layers, shaping as desired.

face

Make a French knot at the perfect spot for each eye with your chosen color (dark brown for dog shown).

Add a small st at the center of each knot with black to accent eyes, if desired. With chosen color (black for dog shown), embroider the nose in satin stitch. With tongue color (pink for dog shown) and using crochet hook to assist, if desired, pick up 3 sts at the perfect spot for the tongue. Work in St st for the desired length with the purl side facing upward so the tongue will curl in at the sides, then BO all tongue sts. Weave in ends.

jacket

Make your toy pup this stylish, ultramini version of the Snazzy Jacket!

jacket

With CC and smaller needles, loosely CO 10 sts. Work in St st, shaping lower edge as foll: CO 2 sts at beg of next 2 rows—14 sts. Inc 1 st at each end of next 2 rows—18 sts. Work 1 row even. Inc 1 st at each end of next row—22 sts. Work 2 rows even, then rep the last inc row once more—20 sts, piece meas about 1¾" (4.5 cm) from CO. Work even in St st until piece meas 3" (7.5 cm) from CO, ending with a WS row. On the next row (RS), make one buttonhole as foll: K1, k2tog, yo, knit to end. Work 1 row even on WS. Inc 1 st at each end of next row, then work 3 rows even—24 sts. Rep the last 4 rows 1 more time—26 sts; piece meas about 5" (12.5 cm) from CO.

shape neck

Work 10 sts, join a second ball of yarn, BO center 6 sts, work to end—10 sts at each side. Working each side separately, dec 1 st at each neck edge every row 3 times, then dec 1 st at each neck edge every other row 2 times—5 sts at each side. On the next RS row, make a buttonhole on the right collar extension (the first section you come to on the RS) as foll: K2, k2tog, yo, k1. Work even for 2 more rows after the buttonhole row. BO all sts loosely.

edge trim

Using crochet hook, work a row of single crochet all around the outer edge of the jacket.

bellyband

Fold the jacket in half down the vertical centerline. On the left side of jacket (the side without buttonholes), mark a position to match the buttonhole using a scrap of contrasting yarn. With WS facing, using crochet hook to assist if desired, pick up 6 sts along the jacket selvedge centered over the marker. Work in St st until bellyband meas 5" (12.5 cm) from pickup row, or desired length plus 1" (2.5 cm) overlap. Loosely BO all sts.

finishing

Weave in all ends on WS. Sew buttons in place on bellyband and on collar extension, or wherever the best fit is achieved. Please attach your buttons very securely to prevent the baby or dog from swallowing them.

knit and stay!

KNITTING FOR POOCHES

snazzy jacket

BASIC DOG JACKET

fun, fast, stylish! The Snazzy Jacket is the basic pattern for all the dog jackets in this book. Make it, and you will be able to make them all. It's worked in a bulky yarn on big needles, so you'll be done in a flash, and you'll be able to fulfill all the requests you get from your friends, who will be envious of your pooch's stylish ways. Shown here in an acrylic/wool blend, the Snazzy Jacket is as easy to care for as it is to knit.

FINISHED SIZE
Small (medium, large); shown in small and medium.

FINISHED MEASUREMENTS
Length from collar to base of tail: 8 (12, 17)", 20.5 (30.5, 43) cm
Rib cage circumference (buttoned): 14½ (22, 31½)"; 37 (56, 80) cm

MATERIALS
Yarn: 65 (155, 290) yards (60 [140, 265] meters) bulky weight machine-washable wool that knits to correct gauge.
Shown in Reynolds Bulky Signature (80% acrylic, 20% wool; 103 yards [94 meters]/100 grams), #360 purple, and Cascade Yarns Chunky Tweed (90% wool, 10% Donegal Tweed;), #603 orange.
Needles: Size US 10½ (6.5 mm) straight needles, or size to obtain gauge.
Size US 10½ (6.5 mm) 29" (70-cm) circular needle (circ) for applying knit-on/bound-off trim as shown (optional).
Notions: Three ¾" (1.9-cm) buttons, measuring tape, yarn needle, scissors, safety pins or scraps of contrasting waste yarn, crochet hook size J/10 (6 mm) (optional).
Gauge: 12 sts and 16 rows = 4" (10 cm) in stockinette stitch (St st). Check your gauge before you begin.

special techniques

k1f&b (knit into front and back of same st)

Knit the stitch to be increased in the usual manner, but do not remove the old stitch from the LH needle. Instead, insert the RH needle into the back of the same stitch and knit it again. Then, remove the old stitch from the LH needle, and you will have two stitches from one stitch.

two-row buttonhole for bellyband (worked over two rows)

Row 1: (RS) K2, BO 2 sts, knit to end of row.
Row 2: (WS) Purl to the gap created by the BO sts in the previous row, loosely CO 2 sts (the same number you bound off) over the gap, purl to end of row.

jacket

Loosely CO 9 (13, 18) sts. Purl 1 row on WS. Working in stockinette stitch (St st), and using the knitting-on method (see page 102), CO 2 (3, 4) sts at the beg of the next 4 rows—17 (25, 34) sts. Increase Row: (RS) Inc 1 st at each side by working k1f&b in the first and last st of the row—19 (27, 36) sts. Work 4 (2, 1) row(s) even. Rep the last 5 (3, 2) rows 1 (2, 4) more time(s), then work the inc row once more—23 (33, 46) sts; piece meas about 4" (10 cm) from CO. Work even in St st until piece meas 4½ (6, 9)" (11.5 [15, 23] cm) from CO, or 3½ (6, 8)" (9 [15, 20.5] cm) less than desired length from collar to base of tail, ending with a WS row. The standard length from collar to base of tail for this pattern is 8 (12, 17)" (20.5 [30.5, 43] cm). Beg with the next RS row, make a two-row buttonhole for the bellyband, as given above. Work even until 1½ (2, 2½)" (3.8 [5, 6.5] cm) above previous button-hole, ending with a WS row. Work another buttonhole the same as the first. Work even until piece meas 6¾ (9, 12½)" (17 [23, 31.5] cm) from CO, or about 1¼ (3, 4½)" (3.2 [7.5, 11.5] cm) less than desired length from base of tail to collar, ending with a WS row.

Shape Midsection:

K1f&b at each end of next RS row, then every 2 rows 2 (5, 8) more times—29 (45, 64) sts. Work even in St st, if necessary, until piece meas about 8 (12, 17)" (20.5 [30.5, 43] cm) from CO, ending with a WS row.

Shape Neck:

Knit across 13 (20, 28) sts, join a second ball of yarn, BO center 3 (5, 8) sts, knit to end—13 (20, 28) sts at each side. Working each side separately, BO 3 (0, 0) sts at each neck edge 1 (0, 0) time(s), then dec 1 st at each neck edge every row 3 (7, 10) times, then dec 1 st at each neck edge every other row 0 (2, 4) times—7 (11, 14) sts at each side. Work even in St st, if neces-sary, until piece meas 1¼ (3¾, 5)" (3.2 [9.5, 12.5] cm) above center neck BO, about 9¼ (15¾, 22)" (23.5 [40, 56] cm) from CO, or desired length, ending with a WS row. Beg with the next RS row, make a two-row buttonhole on the right collar extension (the first sec-tion you come to on the RS) as foll: K3 (5, 6), BO the next 2 sts, k2 (4, 6). On the next row, CO 2 sts over gap in previous row to complete buttonhole. Working each side separately, dec 1 st at each end of each collar extension on the next 2 rows—3 (7, 10) sts at each side. BO all sts loosely.

edge trim

With RS facing, using crochet hook, work a row of single crochet all around the outer edge of the jacket. For an alternate trim method, work the knit-on/bound-off method as foll: With circ needle and RS facing, using crochet hook to assist if desired, pick up and knit a row of sts all the way around the outer edge of the jacket, picking up approximately 4 sts for every 5 rows along the vertical edges, and 1 st for every st

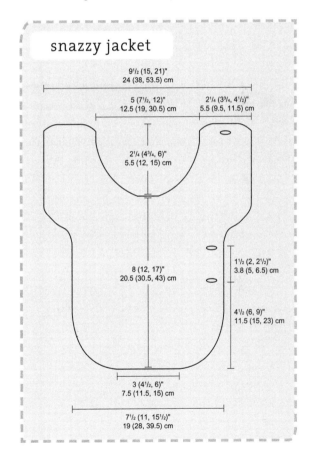

snazzy jacket

9½ (15, 21)"
24 (38, 53.5) cm

5 (7½, 12)"
12.5 (19, 30.5) cm

2¼ (3¾, 4½)"
5.5 (9.5, 11.5) cm

2¼ (4¾, 6)"
5.5 (12, 15) cm

1½ (2, 2½)"
3.8 (5, 6.5) cm

8 (12, 17)"
20.5 (30.5, 43) cm

4½ (6, 9)"
11.5 (15, 23) cm

3 (4½, 6)"
7.5 (11.5, 15) cm

7½ (11, 15½)"
19 (28, 39.5) cm

going across the rows. Do not turn. Working in the same direction, as if working in the round, BO all sts loosely.

bellyband

Try the jacket on your dog and measure the desired length for the bellyband. Depending on the dog's size, knit the bellyband longer or shorter as needed to wrap comfortably around the rib cage, plus 1" (2.5 cm) for the buttonhole overlap. The standard bellyband for this pattern is 8 (12, 17)" (20.5 [30.5, 43] cm) long and 2½ (3, 3½)" (6.5 [7.5, 9] cm) wide.

Fold the jacket in half down the vertical centerline. On the left side of jacket (the side without buttonholes), mark positions matching buttonholes using safety pins or scrap yarn. Place another set of mark-ers outside the first set, each ½" (1.3 cm) away from the first set of markers; the second set of markers should be about 2½ (3, 3½)" (6.5 [7.5, 9] cm) apart. With WS facing, using crochet hook to assist if desired, pick up 8 (9, 11) sts along the jacket selvedge between the outer markers. Work in St st until belly-band meas 8 (12, 17)" (20.5 [30.5, 43] cm) from pickup row, or desired length plus 1" (2.5 cm) over-lap. Loosely BO all sts.

finishing

Weave in all ends on WS. Sew buttons in place on bellyband and collar extension, wherever the best fit is achieved. Please attach your buttons very securely to prevent your dog from swallowing them.

snazzy jacket with faux fur

BASIC DOG JACKET WITH FUR TRIM

a fun and easy-to-knit variation on the Snazzy Jacket. The modification—the addition of a novelty yarn trim—opens up a whole world of possibilities. You can make this jacket downtown funky or uptown classic by simply mixing and matching. Perhaps you would like a multicolor main yarn and a solid fur trim? Or perhaps you'd like to edge your Snazzy Jacket with a different novelty yarn entirely? With all the funky yarns and fibers available, there really is no limit to the possibilities. Your pup may end up with a whole wardrobe of these, a jacket to suit every mood!

FINISHED SIZE
Small (medium, large); shown in size medium.

FINISHED MEASUREMENTS
Length from collar to base of tail: 8 (12, 17)"; 20.5 (30.5, 43) cm
Rib cage circumference (buttoned): 14½ (22, 31½)"; 37 (56, 80) cm

MATERIALS
Yarn: 65 (155, 290) yards (60 [140, 265] meters) bulky weight machine-washable wool that knits to correct gauge in main color (MC); 25 (40, 50) yards (23 [36, 45] meters) of contrasting fur-type yarn for edging (CC).

Shown in Reynolds Bulky Signature (80% acrylic, 20% wool; 103 yards [94 meters]/100 grams), #360 purple (MC), and Crystal Palace Splash (100% polyester; 85 yards [78 meters]/100 grams), #7187 orchid (CC).
Needles: Size US 10½ (6.5 mm) straight needles, or size to obtain gauge.
Size US 10½ (6.5 mm) 29" (70-cm) circular needle (circ) for applying knit-on/bound-off trim as shown (optional).
Notions: Three ¾" (1.9-cm) buttons, measuring tape, yarn needle, scissors, safety pins or scraps of contrasting waste yarn, crochet hook size J/10 (6 mm) (optional).
Gauge: 12 sts and 16 rows = 4" (10 cm) in stockinette stitch (St st). Check your gauge before you begin.

jacket

Using MC, work exactly as for the basic Snazzy Jacket (see page 53) until the Edge Trim.

edge trim

With circ needle, RS facing, and CC, using crochet hook to assist if desired, pick up and knit a row of sts all the way around the outer edge of the jacket, picking up approximately 4 sts for every 5 rows along the vertical edges, and 1 st for every st going across the rows. Do not turn. Join for working in the round and knit 2 rounds. BO all sts loosely.

bellyband and finishing

Work exactly the same as for the basic Snazzy Jacket, using MC for the bellyband. See the diagram for the basic Snazzy Jacket on page 55 for finished dimensions.

Consider making the bellyband a different color to create an even more playful garment. This can be a fun way to use leftover yarns in your stash!

inside-out jacket

TEXTURED DOG JACKET

the Inside-Out Jacket can be worked in any textured yarn or combination of yarns that knit to the proper gauge. Shown here in a nubby pink yarn, it has a decidedly "Jackie O" quality. However, work it in a slubby natural tone and it will be quite masculine. Choosing this jacket will allow you to truly take advantage of the textural quality of today's wonderful yarns, because it features reverse stockinette stitch (rev St st); the purl side is considered the "right" (or public) side. Consider experimenting with two yarns held together to create your own unique yarn variation—and knit your own canine couture!

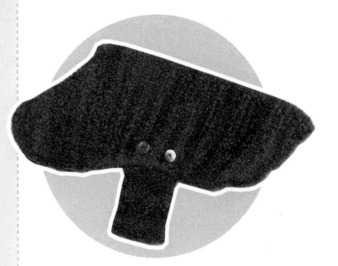

FINISHED SIZE
Small (medium, large); shown in size medium.

FINISHED MEASUREMENTS
Length from collar to base of tail: 8 (12, 17)"; 20.5 (30.5, 43) cm

Rib cage circumference (buttoned): 14½ (22, 31½"; 37 (56, 80) cm

MATERIALS
Yarn: 45 (100, 190) yards (38 [90, 170] meters) bulky weight textured yarn, or combination of yarns, that knits to correct gauge.

If you are using two yarns held together, you will need the amount of yarn shown above for *both* yarns.

Shown in Artful Yarns Circus (95% wool, 5% acrylic; 93 yards [85 meters]/100 grams), #10 side show (pink/purple mix).

Needles: Size US 10½ (6.5 mm) straight needles, or size to obtain gauge.

Notions: Three ¾" (1.9-cm) buttons, measuring tape, yarn needle, scissors, safety pins or scraps of contrasting waste yarn, crochet hook size J/10 (6 mm) (optional).

Gauge: 12 sts and 16 rows = 4" (10 cm) in reverse stockinette stitch (rev St st). Check your gauge before you begin.

special techniques

k1f&b (knit into front and back of same st)

Knit the stitch to be increased in the usual manner, but do not remove the old stitch from the LH needle. Instead, insert the RH needle into the back of the same stitch and knit it again. Then, remove the old stitch from the LH needle, and you will have two stitches from one stitch.

two-row buttonhole for bellyband (worked over two rows)

Row 1: (RS) P2, BO 2 sts, purl to end of row.
Row 2: (WS) Knit to the gap created by the BO sts in the previous row, loosely CO 2 sts (the same number you bound off) over the gap, knit to end of row.

jacket

Loosely CO 9 (13, 18) sts. Knit 1 row on WS. Working in reverse stockinette stitch (rev St st; purl all sts on RS rows, knit all sts on WS rows), and using the knitting-on method (see page 102), CO 2 (3, 4) sts at the beg of the next 4 rows—17 (25, 34) sts. Increase Row: (RS) Inc 1 st at each side by working k1f&b in the first and last st of the row—19 (27, 36) sts. Work 4 (2, 1) row(s) even. Rep the last 5 (3, 2) rows 1 (2, 4) more time(s), then work the inc row once more—23 (33, 46) sts; piece meas about 4" (10 cm) from CO. Work even in St st until piece meas 4½ (6, 9)" (11.5 [15, 23] cm) from CO, or 3½ (6, 8)" (9 [15, 20.5] cm) less than desired length from collar to base of tail, ending with a WS row. The standard length from collar to base of tail for this pattern is 8 (12, 17)" (20.5 [30.5, 43] cm). Beg with the next RS row, make a two-row buttonhole for the bellyband, as given above.

Work even until 1½ (2, 2½)" (3.8 [5, 6.5] cm) above previous buttonhole, ending with a WS row. Work another buttonhole the same as the first. Work even until piece meas 6¾ (9, 12½)" (17 [23, 31.5] cm) from CO, or about 1¼ (3, 4½)" (3.2 [7.5, 11.5] cm) less than desired length from base of tail to collar, ending with a WS row.

shape midsection:

K1f&b at each end of next RS row, then every 2 rows 2 (5, 8) more times—29 (45, 64) sts. Work even in rev St st, if necessary, until piece meas about 8 (12, 17)" (20.5 [30.5, 43] cm) from CO, ending with a WS row.

shape neck:

Purl across 13 (20, 28) sts, join a second ball of yarn, BO center 3 (5, 8) sts, purl to end—13 (20, 28) sts at each side. Working each side separately, BO 3 (0, 0) sts at each neck edge 1 (0, 0) time(s), then dec 1 st at each neck edge every row 3 (7, 10) times, then dec 1 st at each neck edge every other row 0 (2, 4) times—7 (11, 14) sts at each side. Work even in rev St st, if necessary, until piece meas 1¼ (3¾, 5)" (3.2 [9.5, 12.5] cm)

above center neck BO, about 9¼ (15¾, 22)" (23.5 [40, 56] cm) from CO, or desired length, ending with a WS row. Beg with the next RS row, make a two-row buttonhole on the right collar extension (the first section you come to on the RS) as foll: P3 (5, 6), BO the next 2 sts, p2 (4, 6). On the next row, CO 2 sts over gap in previous row to complete buttonhole. Working each side separately, dec 1 st at each end of each collar extension on the next 2 rows—3 (7, 10) sts at each side. BO all sts loosely.

edge trim

With RS facing, using crochet hook, work a row of single crochet all around the outer edge of the jacket. Cut yarn and fasten off last st.

bellyband

Try the jacket on your dog and measure the desired length for the bellyband. Depending on the dog's size, knit the bellyband longer or shorter as needed to wrap comfortably around the rib cage, plus 1" (2.5 cm) for the buttonhole overlap. The standard bellyband for this pattern is 8 (12, 17)" (20.5 [30.5, 43] cm) long and 2½ (3, 3½)" (6.5 [7.5, 9] cm) wide.

Fold the jacket in half down the vertical centerline. On the left side of jacket (the side without buttonholes), mark positions matching buttonholes using safety pins or scrap yarn. Place another set of markers outside the first set, each ½" (1.3 cm) away from the first set of markers; the second set of markers should be about 2½ (3, 3½)" (6.5 [7.5, 9] cm) apart. With WS facing, using crochet hook to assist if desired, pick up 8 (9, 11) sts along the jacket selvedge between the outer markers. Work in rev St st until bellyband meas 8 (12, 17)" (20.5 [30.5, 43] cm) from pickup row, or desired length plus 1" (2.5 cm) overlap. Loosely BO all sts.

finishing

Weave in all ends on WS. Sew buttons in place on bellyband and collar extension, wherever the best fit is achieved. Please attach your buttons very securely to prevent your dog from swallowing them. See the diagram for the basic Snazzy Jacket on page 55 for finished dimensions.

puppy pullover

EASY DOG PULLOVER

the Puppy Pullover takes advantage of a dog's familiarity with having a collar placed over its head (a sure sign of a W-A-L-K!) This garment slips easily over the head and buttons behind the front legs—no wrestling squirmy pups into leg holes. Worked in basic stockinette stitch with basic knit one, purl one rib, this sweater is simple to knit, but features a lot of details in the directions. It is a good choice for knitters who want to advance their technique and their pattern reading skills. While the back is shaped in the same way as the other jackets included in this collection, there is a bit of shaping for the T-shaped belly piece, but nothing too hard. The first time you sew this together, it might seem like it's going to be sweater origami, but stick with it; there are only two simple seams to sew. Once you get the pieces laid out properly it's a snap.

Shown here in an easy-care cotton/acrylic blend, this project works up fast at a large gauge on big needles. Tips for customizing the fit are found throughout the pattern.

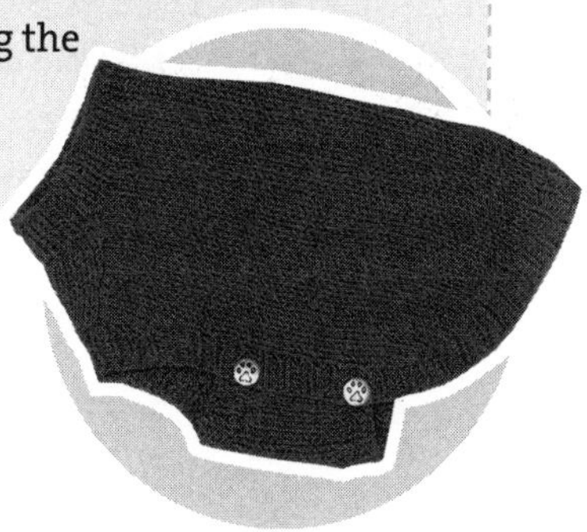

FINISHED SIZE
Small (medium, large); shown in size medium.

FINISHED MEASUREMENTS
Length from collar to base of tail: 8 (12, 17)"; 20.5 (30.5, 43) cm, not including ribbed trim
Rib cage circumference (buttoned): 14½ (22½, 31½)" (37 [57, 80] cm), including ribbed trim

MATERIALS
Yarn: 115 (240, 440) yards (105 [220, 402] meters) bulky yarn that knits to correct gauge.

Shown in Muench Goa (50% cotton, 50% acrylic; 66 yards [60 meters]/50 grams), #42 pomegranate.
Needles: Size US 10 (6 mm) straight needles, or size to obtain gauge.
Size US 8 (5 mm) 16" (40-cm) and 29" (70-cm) circular needles (circ) for applying ribbed edgings.
Notions: Four ⅞" (2.2-cm) buttons, measuring tape, yarn needle, scissors, safety pins, scraps of contrasting waste yarn, stitch marker, crochet hook size J/10 (6 mm) (optional).
Gauge: 13 sts and 18 rows = 4" (10 cm) in stockinette stitch (St st). Check your gauge before you begin.

special techniques

k1f&b (knit into front and back of same st)

Knit the stitch to be increased in the usual manner, but do not remove the old stitch from the LH needle. Instead, insert the RH needle into the back of the same stitch and knit it again. Then, remove the old stitch from the LH needle, and you will have two stitches from one stitch.

two-row buttonhole

Row 1: *Work in rib patt to marked position, BO 2 sts; rep from * 3 more times, work in rib patt to end.

Row 2: *Work in rib patt to gap created by the BO sts in the previous row, loosely CO 2 sts (the same number you bound off) over the gap; rep from * 3 more times, work in rib patt to end.

back

With straight needles, loosely CO 10 (20, 36) sts. Working in stockinette stitch (St st), and using the knitting-on method (see page 102), CO 2 sts at the beg of the next 2 rows (all sizes)—14 (24, 40) sts. Increase Row: (RS) Inc 1 st at each side by working k1f&b in the first and last st of the row—16 (26, 42) sts. Work 1 (1, 2) row(s) even. Rep the last 2 (2, 3) rows 1 (3, 2) more time(s), then work the inc row once more—20 (34, 48) sts; piece meas about 1½ (2½, 2¾)" (3.8 [6.5, 7] cm) from CO. Work even in St st until piece meas 5¾ (8¾, 12)" (14.5 [22, 30.5] cm) from CO edge, or 2¼ (3¼, 5)" (5.5 [8.5, 12.5] cm) less than desired length from collar to base of tail, ending with a WS row.

customization tip

The standard length from collar to base of tail for this pattern is 8 (12, 17)" (20.5 [30.5, 43] cm), without the ribbed trim. So, for example, if your dog needs a size medium with a 10" (25.5-cm) length from collar to base of tail, you would work even until the piece meas 6¾" (17 cm) from CO edge.

chunky jacket

fancy
chunky
jacket

faux fur cardigan

21st-century
matinee set

pawprints
cardigan

infant
gift set

toy dog

snake cables
pullover

baby
gift
basket

snazzy
jacket

snazzy jacket
(mini!)

snazzy jacket with faux fur

inside out jacket

puppy
pullover

luck-of-the-irish
blanket

luck-of-the-irish
jacket

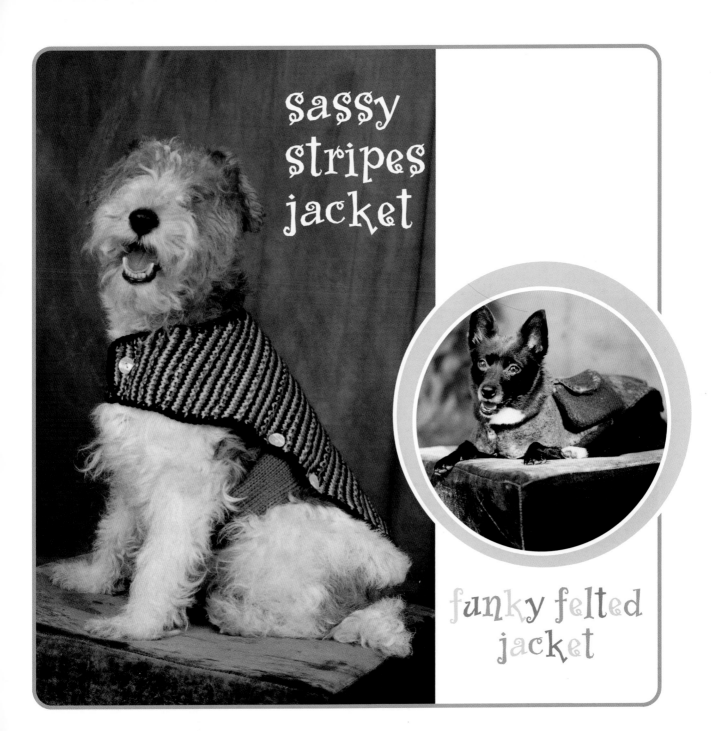

sassy
stripes
jacket

funky felted
jacket

dog gift basket with toy bones

Beg with the next RS row, work shoulder shaping as foll: K1f&b at each end of next RS row, then work 4 (3, 4) rows even. Rep the last 0 (4, 5) rows 0 (2, 2) more time(s)—22 (40, 54) sts. Inc 1 st at each of next RS row, then every other row 1 (0, 2) more time(s)—26 (42, 60) sts. Work 1 row even; piece meas about 8 (12, 17)" 20.5 (30.5, 43] cm) or desired length from CO. Loosely BO all sts.

front

With straight needles, loosely CO 20 (34, 48) sts. Work even in St st for 1½ (3, 3¾)" (3.8 [7.5, 9.5] cm). At the beg of the next 2 rows, BO 6 (11, 16) sts—8 (12, 16) sts.

customization tip

If your dog is slender, you can make an adjustment to the underbelly band by casting on fewer sts and working fewer rows before the bind offs. You can also work the pattern as given and adjust for a more snug fit by the placement of the buttons on the front of the finished garment.

Beg shaping for chest and front leg holes as foll: Dec 1 st at each end every 2 (3, 6) rows 2 times—4 (8, 12) sts. Work even for 4 (6, 8) rows; piece meas about 3½ (6¼, 8½)" (9 [16, 21.5] cm) from CO, or 2½ (3¾, 6½)" (6.5 [9, 16.5] cm) less than desired length to base of neck.

customization tip

The standard length from base of the neck to the end of the front piece for this pattern is 6 (10, 15)" (15 [25.5, 38] cm), without the ribbed trim. Measure your dog's chest from the base of the collar, down along the breastbone, between the front legs, and along the underside of the belly to the end of the rib cage. If your dog needs an extra inch or so, work that many extra rows here. If your dog needs less length, omit some or all of the 4 (6, 8) rows worked even at the end of the decreases above.

Cont to shape chest and front leg holes as foll: Inc 1 st at each end of the next row, then every 2 (2, 3) rows 2 (5, 7) more times—10 (20, 28) sts. Work 5 (5, 6) rows even, then work inc row once more—12 (22, 30) sts; piece meas about 6 (10, 15)" (15 [25.5, 38] cm) from CO.

shape neck:

On the next RS row, knit across 3 (6, 9) sts, join a second ball of yarn, BO center 6 (10, 12) sts, knit to end—3 (6, 9) sts at each side. Working each side separately, dec 1 st at each neck edge every row 2 (3, 4) times—1 (3, 5) st(s) at each side. On the next row, inc 1 st at outside edges *only*, not at the neck edges—2 (4, 6) sts at each side. Dec 1 st at each neck edge every row 1 (3, 5) more time(s)—1 st at each side. Cut yarn and draw through last St at each side.

assembly

Lay the back on a table with the WS (purl) side facing up. With safety pins or contrasting scrap yarn, mark two positions along bound-off edge of back, 1¾ (2¾, 4¼" (4.5 [7, 11] cm) in from each end, as shown by colored lines on diagram. Lay the front on top of the back with its RS (knit) side facing up. On the front, measure down 1¾ (2¾, 4¼)" (4.5 [7, 11] cm) from the last st along each outside edge, as shown on diagram. With wrong sides touching, swivel the front, or fold down a triangular flap from the back, as required to align the markers at each shoulder, matching the dotted seams as shown on diagram. Sew the shoulder seams. Weave in ends on WS.

neckband

With shorter circ needle and RS facing, using crochet hook to assist, if desired, pick up and knit 30 (50, 68) sts evenly around neck opening as foll: 6 (9, 13) sts along left side of front neck, 4 (8, 10) sts across BO sts at center front, 6 (9, 13) sts along right side of front neck, 14 (24, 32) sts across back neck. Join for working in the round (rnd), and place marker to indicate beg of

rnd. Work in k1, p1 rib for 1½" (3.8 cm) or desired length. BO all sts very loosely in patt. Use larger straight needle for binding off if it makes it easier for you to keep the neck edge very elastic.

lower front edge

With either circ needle and RS facing, using crochet hook to assist, if desired, pick up and knit 20 (32, 46) sts along the cast on edge of front. Work in k1, p1 rib for 1" (2.5 cm). BO all sts loosely in patt.

outer edge

Try the jacket on your dog, wrapping the front between the front legs to meet up with the back at each side. Temporarily pin the front to the back, letting the two pieces gap by the length of the safety pin to account for the width of the rib trim. The positions for 4 buttons on the front are shown as black circles on the

Consider working the neck trim longer for a turtleneck, or even longer for a snood; or try a rolled St st edge by knitting every round for the desired length.

diagram, at the corners of the lower front. When the outer edge trim has been applied, the buttons will be attached to the corners where they abut the trim. With more safety pins or scrap yarn, mark 4 corresponding buttonhole positions on the edges of the back on both sides, aiming for the best possible fit. Remove the jacket from the dog, and adjust the buttonhole markers to be symmetrical, if necessary. Place another safety pin or piece of scrap yarn in the center of the CO edge of back.

With longer circ needle and RS facing, using crochet hook to assist, if desired, pick up and knit 100 (148, 220) sts around outer edge of jacket from corner A to corner B as foll: 18 (28, 42) sts from corner A to shoulder seam, 32 (46, 68) sts from shoulder seam to center of back CO edge, 32 (46, 68) sts from center of back CO edge to other shoulder seam, 18 (28, 42) sts from shoulder seam to corner B.

customization tip:

If you have made length adjustments, your edging will have a different number of sts. Pick up and knit about 3 sts for every 4 rows

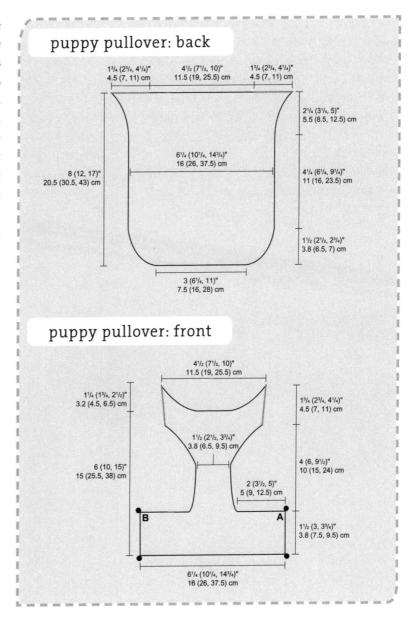

along side edges, and 1 st for each st across the rows, making sure that you pick up an even number of sts.

Work outer edge in k1, p1 rib for 2 rows. On the next 2 rows, cont in rib patt, and make 4 buttonholes as given in the two-row buttonhole method above. Work 2 more rows in rib patt. BO all sts loosely in patt.

lower sides

With shorter circ needle and RS facing, using crochet hook to assist, if desired, pick up and knit 9 (18, 22) sts along straight selvedge of lower front. Work in k1, p1 rib for 5 rows. BO all sts loosely in patt. Work other side of lower front in the same manner.

finishing

Weave in all ends on WS. Sew buttons in place at corners of lower front as shown on diagram, or wherever the best fit is achieved. Please attach your buttons very securely to prevent your dog from swallowing them.

luck-of-the-irish jacket

ARAN DOG JACKET

cables are not hard to knit, and the Aran cable stitchwork you'll use to create this Luck-of-the-Irish Jacket is a great way to show off (or advance) your knitting skills. The horseshoe cables are a simple variation of a basic rope cable. When two rope cables are paired up side by side and turned in opposite directions, they create the optical illusion of a horseshoe, a pattern that is sometimes called claw cables. Like so many textured and cable stitches, they look much harder to create than they really are. Impress yourself and your friends with this project. At a gauge of four stitches to the inch you'll be done in no time, and your pup will thank you for this lovely jacket on the first chilly day of fall. Remember, cables are not hard to knit! Once you master the simple technique of using a cable needle this project will be a breeze.

FINISHED SIZE
Small (medium, large); shown in size medium.

FINISHED MEASUREMENTS
Length from collar to base of tail: 8 (12, 17)"; 20.5 (30.5, 43) cm

Rib cage circumference (buttoned): 14½ (22, 31½)", 37 (56, 80) cm

MATERIALS
Yarn: 105 (220, 380) yards (95 [200, 350] meters) bulky weight machine-washable wool that knits to correct gauge.

Shown in Brown Sheep Company Lamb's Pride Superwash Bulky (100% machine-washable wool; 110 yards [100 meters]/100 grams), #SW115 oats n' cream.

Needles: Size US 10 (6 mm) straight needles, or size to obtain gauge.

Size US 10 (6 mm) 29" (70-cm) circular needle (circ) for applying knit-on/bound-off trim.

Notions: Three ¾" (1.9-cm) buttons, cable needle, measuring tape, yarn needle, scissors, safety pins or scraps of contrasting waste yarn, stitch markers (optional), crochet hook size J/10 (6 mm) (optional).

Gauge: 14 sts and 24 rows = 4" (10 cm) in seed st; 20-st cable panel from chart = 4" (10 cm) wide. Check your gauge before you begin.

special techniques

k1f&b (knit into front and back of same st)

Knit the stitch to be increased in the usual manner, but do not remove the old stitch from the LH needle. Instead, insert the RH needle into the back of the same stitch and knit it again. Then, remove the old stitch from the LH needle, and you will have two stitches from one stitch.

two-row buttonhole for bellyband (worked over two rows)

Row 1: (RS) Work 2 sts in patt, BO 2 sts, work in patt to end of row.

Row 2: (WS) Work in patt to the gap created by the BO sts in the previous row, loosely CO 2 sts (the same number you bound off) over the gap, work in patt to end of row.

seed stitch (odd number of sts)

All Rows: *K1, p1; rep from * to last st, end k1.

seed stitch (even number of sts)

Row 1: *K1, p1; rep from * to end.

All Other Rows: Purl the knit sts, and knit the purl sts as they appear.

reading charts

If you need additional help reading the chart used for this pattern, see page 107.

jacket

Loosely CO 20 sts. On the next row (RS), work Row 1 of Aran jacket chart (see page 72). Cont in patt from chart (rep Rows 1–8 for patt), and *at the same time*, use the knitting-on method (see page 102) to CO 2 (3, 5)

sts at the beg of the next 2 (4, 4) rows, working sts added at each side in seed st as they become established—24 (32, 40) sts. Note: You may find it helpful to use stitch markers to set off the center 20 sts to be worked from the chart. Increase Row: (RS) Inc 1 st at each side by working k1f&b in the first and last st of the row—26 (34, 42) sts. Work 6 (3, 1) row(s) even. Rep the last 7 (4, 2) rows 2 (4, 8) more time(s), then work the inc row once more—32 (44, 60) sts; piece meas about 4" (10 cm) from CO. Work even in St st until piece meas 4½ (6, 9)" (11.5 [15, 23] cm) from CO, or 3½ (6, 8)" (9 [15, 20.5] cm) less than desired length from collar to base of tail, ending with a WS row. The standard length from collar to base of tail for this pattern is 8 (12, 17)" (20.5 [30.5, 43] cm). Beg with the next RS row, make a two-row buttonhole for bellyband, as given above.

Sometimes called "fisherman knitting," Aran knitting is the traditional cabled knitting of Ireland and is named for the Aran Islands, the three tiny islands off Ireland's southwest coast where this richly textured type of knitting developed. The culture of the Islands was a fishing culture, and the inhabitants traveled up and down the Atlantic coast following their catch and meeting other fishermen from all over Western Europe.

This knitting style is at once uniquely Irish, but with global appeal. The Aran technique is a unique blend of native knitting skill, the influence of Celtic art and culture, and techniques learned from sharing ideas and motifs with knitters from other cultures. In fact, it is thought that much of what we now know as Aran knitting was brought back to the islands by knitters who had traveled to America and came home to share the skills they picked up while abroad.

The hallmark of the Aran knitting style is the use of deep, sculptural cable panels combined with textured fill stitches. Steeped in folklore (in classic Irish fashion), every stitch pattern is said to have a story, and the stitches used in these projects are no exception. The seed stitch, known in Aran knitting as moss stitch, represents the seaweed collected from the Aran beaches and hauled up the cliffs to the islanders' small fields. There, it is mixed with clay and to enrich the local soil, and so symbolizes fertility and prosperity. The cables evoke the ropes used by the fishermen to haul in their nets and are said to bring luck to the wearer. For further reading on Aran knitting and folklore, see the Sources and Further Reading on page 111.

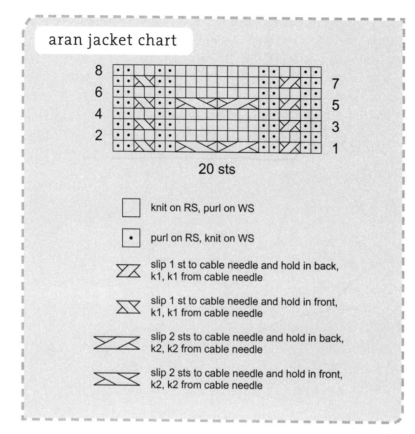

aran jacket chart

```
8                                        7
6                                        5
4
2                                        3
                                         1
```

20 sts

☐ knit on RS, purl on WS

▪ purl on RS, knit on WS

slip 1 st to cable needle and hold in back,
k1, k1 from cable needle

slip 1 st to cable needle and hold in front,
k1, k1 from cable needle

slip 2 sts to cable needle and hold in back,
k2, k2 from cable needle

slip 2 sts to cable needle and hold in front,
k2, k2 from cable needle

Shape Midsection:

K1f&b at each end of next RS row, then every 3 rows 3 (3, 6) times, then every 2 rows 0 (3, 3) times—40 (58, 80) sts. Work even in St st, if necessary, until piece meas about 8 (12, 17)" (20.5 [30.5, 43] cm) from CO, ending with a WS row.

Shape Neck:

Knit across 16 (24, 33) sts, join a second ball of yarn, BO center 8 (10, 14) sts, knit to end—16 (24, 33) sts at each side. Working each side separately, BO 3 (0, 0) sts at each neck edge 1 (0, 0) time(s), then dec 1 st at each neck edge every row 5 (0, 3) times, then dec 1 st at each neck edge every other row 0 (11, 14) times—8 (13, 16) sts at each side. Work even in patt, if necessary, until piece meas 1¼ (3¾, 5)" (3.2 [9.5, 12.5] cm) above center neck BO, about 9¼ (15¾, 22)" (23.5 [40, 56] cm) from CO, or desired length, ending with a WS row. Beg with the next RS row, make a two-row buttonhole on the right collar extension (the first section you come to on the RS) as foll: Work 3 (6, 7) sts in patt, BO the next 2 sts, work 3 (5, 7) sts in patt. On the next row, CO 2 sts over gap in previous row to complete buttonhole. Working each side separately, work 2 rows even, then dec 1 st at each end of each collar extension on the next 2 rows—4 (9, 12) sts at each side. BO all sts loosely.

Work even until 1½ (2, 2½)" (3.8 [5, 6.5] cm) above previous buttonhole, ending with a WS row. Work another buttonhole the same as the first. Work even until piece meas 6¾ (9, 12½)" (17 [23, 31.5] cm) from CO, or about 1¼ (3, 4½)" (3.2 [7.5, 11.5] cm) less than desired length from base of tail to collar, ending with a WS row.

edge trim

With circ needle and RS facing, using crochet hook to assist if desired, pick up and knit a row of sts all the way around the outer edge of the jacket, picking up approximately 3 or 4 sts alternately for every 6 rows along the vertical edges, and 1 st for every st going across the rows. Do not turn. Join for working in the round and knit 6 rounds for a rolled edge. BO all sts loosely. For neat, simple alternate edge trim, pick up sts as given above, but then immediately BO all sts on the next row.

bellyband

Try the jacket on your dog and measure the desired length for the bellyband. Depending on the dog's size, knit the bellyband longer or shorter as needed to wrap comfortably around the rib cage, plus 1" (2.5 cm) for the buttonhole overlap. The standard bellyband for this pattern is 8 (12, 17)" (20.5 [30.5, 43] cm) long and 2½ (3, 3½)" (6.5 [7.5, 9] cm) wide.

Fold the jacket in half down the vertical centerline. On the left side of jacket (the side without buttonholes), mark positions matching buttonholes using safety pins

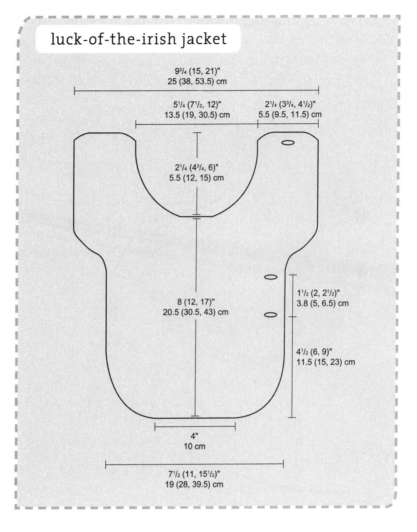

luck-of-the-irish jacket

9¾ (15, 21)"
25 (38, 53.5) cm

5¼ (7½, 12)"
13.5 (19, 30.5) cm

2¼ (3¾, 4½)"
5.5 (9.5, 11.5) cm

2¼ (4¾, 6)"
5.5 (12, 15) cm

8 (12, 17)"
20.5 (30.5, 43) cm

1½ (2, 2½)"
3.8 (5, 6.5) cm

4½ (6, 9)"
11.5 (15, 23) cm

4"
10 cm

7½ (11, 15½)"
19 (28, 39.5) cm

or scrap yarn. Place another set of markers outside the first set, each ½" (1.3 cm) away from the first set of markers; the second set of markers should be about 2½ (3, 3½)" (6.5 [7.5, 9] cm) apart. With WS facing, using crochet hook to assist if desired, pick up 9 (11, 13) sts along the jacket selvedge between the outer markers.

Work in seed st until bellyband meas 8 (12, 17)" (20.5 [30.5, 43] cm) from pickup row, or desired length plus 1" (2.5 cm) overlap. Loosely BO all sts.

finishing

Weave in all ends on WS. Sew buttons in place on bellyband and collar extension, wherever the best fit is achieved. Please attach your buttons very securely to prevent your dog from swallowing them.

luck-of-the-irish blanket

ARAN DOG BLANKET

coupled with the Luck-of-the-Irish Jacket, this blanket makes a magnificent gift set for a friend's new puppy, or a delightful indulgence for your own furry baby. Just like the jacket, the simple cable motif features panels of seed stitch accompanied by wide horseshoe cables, which are worked here in alternating directions for a little added flair. With no shaping to worry about, this project is perfect for a knitter new to Aran cabling who would like to focus on working different stitch patterns across a row. Although designed for a pooch, it makes a fantastic gift for a two-legged baby as well.

I recommend you use a circular needle to knit this project. Although it is worked flat (knitted back and forth in rows instead of round and round), the circular needle can carry enough stitches for the full width of the project, and it allows the weight of the growing blanket to rest in your lap, instead of being supported out to the side as with straight needles. For more information, see "Knitting Flat on Circular Needles" on page 103.

FINISHED SIZE
About 28" (71 cm) square.

MATERIALS
Yarn: 675 yards (620 meters) bulky weight machine-washable wool that knits to correct gauge.
Shown in Brown Sheep Company Lamb's Pride Superwash Bulky (100% machine-washable wool; 110 yards [100 meters]/100 grams), #SW115 oats n' cream.

Needles: Size US 10 (6 mm) 29" (70-cm) circular needle (circ), or size to obtain gauge.
Notions: Cable needle, measuring tape, yarn needle, scissors, stitch markers (optional).
Gauge: 14 sts and 24 rows = 4" (10 cm) in seed st; 20-st cable panel from chart = 4" (10 cm) wide. Check your gauge before you begin.

STARTING AND ENDING CABLE PANELS

When you cross the stitches for a cable, you are temporarily producing a double thickness of fabric. For example, in a basic four-stitch rope cable, when you work the crossing row and hold the stitches to the front or back, you are essentially stacking two groups of stitches on top of each other, changing a section of the knitting that was one-layer thick and four stitches wide to two layers thick and two stitches wide. Because of this, cable panels contract widthwise, and usually pack more stitches into each inch than a one-layer fabric.

When a cable panel changes to a noncabled pattern, the cable stitches relax sideways into a single layer of fabric, and you may find that the fabric flares noticeably above the cable. Likewise, when a group of stitches changes from a single layer fabric to a cable, the cable draws in, and the stitches below the cable appear to flare out. One way to create a smooth transition to and from cables is to change the number of stitches where the patterns change. When beginning a cable you can increase a few stitches, and at the top of a cable you can decrease a few stitches. In this pattern, the number of stitches changes at the cable transitions, allowing the seed stitch border at the top and bottom of the blanket to lie flat and smooth.

special techniques

seed stitch (odd number of sts)
All Rows: *K1, p1; rep from * to last st, end k1.

seed stitch (even number of sts)
Row 1: *K1, p1; rep from * to end.
All Other Rows: Purl the knit sts, and knit the purl sts as they appear.

make 1 (m1):
With the tip of the LH needle inserted from front to back, pick up the connecting strand between the two needles and place it on the LH needle. Knit the lifted strand through its back loop, twisting it to avoid leaving a hole.

reading charts
If you need additional help reading the chart used for this pattern, see page 107.

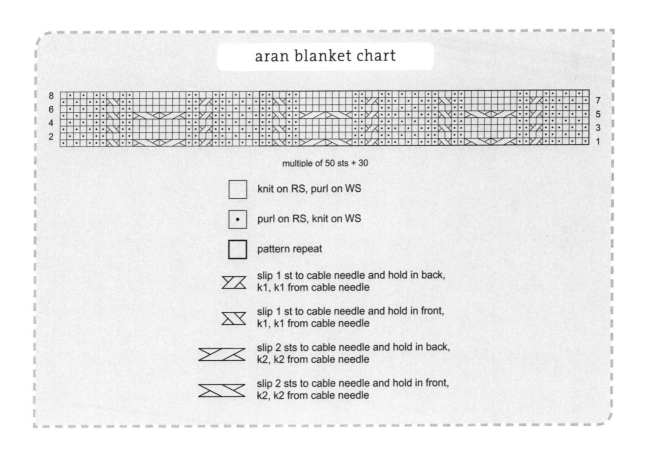

aran blanket chart

multiple of 50 sts + 30

	knit on RS, purl on WS
	purl on RS, knit on WS
	pattern repeat
	slip 1 st to cable needle and hold in back, k1, k1 from cable needle
	slip 1 st to cable needle and hold in front, k1, k1 from cable needle
	slip 2 sts to cable needle and hold in back, k2, k2 from cable needle
	slip 2 sts to cable needle and hold in front, k2, k2 from cable needle

blanket

Loosely CO 120 sts. Work in seed st for 1½" (3.8 cm). On the next row (WS), establish patt and inc as foll: *Work 5 sts seed st, [K2, p2] twice, [p1, m1] twice, [p2, k2] twice; rep from * 4 more times, work 5 sts seed st—130 sts. Change to Aran blanket chart, beg with Row 1 (RS). Cont in patt as established, repeating Rows 1–8 of chart, until piece meas about 26½" (67.5 cm) from CO, ending with a WS row. Note: You may find it help- ful to use stitch markers to set off each repeat of the chart. On the next row (RS), work across in seed st, de- creasing 10 sts by working 2 sts tog twice in patt at the top of each 8-st horseshoe cable—120 sts. Work even in seed st for 1½" (3.8 cm). BO all sts loosely.

finishing

Weave in all ends on WS. Lightly steam block only if necessary (blocking can flatten the rich cable texture you have worked so hard to achieve).

sassy stripes jacket

STRIPED DOG JACKET

this jacket features stripes of three colors, with two of the stripes worked in seed stitch every now and again. Like so many good things in knitting, the Sassy Stripes Jacket looks very impressive and hard to knit, but it's really quite easy. One of the best things about this stitch pattern is the way you can play with it by changing the colors and the order in which you use them. The finished jacket shown here is presented in a muted color combination; look at the idea swatches to see how other color combinations can make this jacket look. Be daring, play around with your own color ideas; any worsted weight yarn will do, but here we've used a super-smooth washable Merino that can't be beat for its softness, ease of care, and fantastic range of mix-and-match colors.

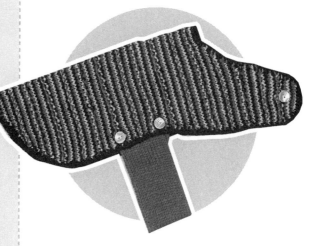

FINISHED SIZE
Small (medium, large); shown in size medium.

FINISHED MEASUREMENTS
Length from collar to base of tail: 8 (12, 17)"; 20.5 (30.5, 43) cm
Rib cage circumference (buttoned): 14½ (22, 31½)"; 37 (56, 80) cm

MATERIALS
Yarn: 65 (135, 185) yards (60 [124, 170] meters) Aran weight wool that knits to correct gauge in color 1 (C1); 45 (85, 150) yards (40 [78, 137] meters) in color 2 (C2); 30 (60, 110) yards (28 [56, 100] meters) in color 3 (C3).

Shown in Mission Falls 1824 Wool (100% machine-washable Merino wool; 85 yards [78 meters]/50 grams), #005 raven (C1), #016 thyme (C2), and #002 stone (C3).
Note: These amounts are sufficient for working the edge trim in C1 and the bellyband in C2; please allow extra yarn if you are experimenting with your own color combinations (always strongly encouraged!)
Needles: Size US 6 (4 mm) straight needles, or size to obtain gauge.
Notions: Three ½" (1.3-cm) buttons, measuring tape, yarn needle, scissors, safety pins or scraps of contrasting waste yarn, crochet hook size G/6 (4 mm) (optional).
Gauge: 19 sts and 26½ rows = 4" (10 cm) in Sassy Stripes pattern. Check your gauge before you begin. *5 sts/in.*

special techniques

k1f&b (knit into front and back of same st)

Knit the stitch to be increased in the usual manner, but do not remove the old stitch from the LH needle. Instead, insert the RH needle into the back of the same stitch and knit it again. Then, remove the old stitch from the LH needle, and you will have two stitches from one stitch.

two-row buttonhole for bellyband (worked over two rows)

Row 1: (RS) Work 2 sts in patt, BO 2 sts, work in patt to end of row.

Row 2: (WS) Work in patt to the gap created by the BO sts in the previous row, loosely CO 2 sts (the same number you bound off) over the gap, work in patt to end of row.

sassy stripes pattern (see chart on page 83)

Row 1: (RS) With C2 knit. *wine*

Row 2: (WS) With C3 purl. *gold*

Row 3: With C1 knit. *blue*

Row 4: With C2 purl. *wine*

Row 5: With C3 knit. *gold*

Row 6: With C1 purl. *blue*

Row 7: With C2, *k1, p1; rep from *, ending k1 if there is an odd number of sts.

Row 8: With C3, purl the knits and knit the purls as they appear to you (seed st).

Rows 9–12: Rep Rows 3–6.

Row 13: With C2 knit. *wine*

Row 14: With C3 purl. *gold*

Row 15: With C1, rep Row 7 *blue*

Row 16: With C2, rep Row 8. *wine*

Row 17: With C3 knit. *gold*

Row 18: With C1 purl.

Row 19: With C2 knit.

Row 20: With C3 purl. *gold*

Row 21: With C1 knit.

Row 22: With C2 purl.

Row 23: With C3, rep Row 7. *gold*

Row 24: With C1, rep Row 8.

Rep Rows 1–24 for patt.

jacket

With C2, loosely CO 14 (22, 31) sts. Work Row 1 of Sassy Stripes patt. Cont in stripe patt, and using the knitting-on method (see page 102) CO 3 (5, 6) sts at the beg of the next 4 rows—26 (42, 55) sts. Increase *7th* Row: (RS) Inc 1 st at each side by working k1f&b in the first and last st of the row, working increased sts into stripe patt as necessary—28 (44, 57) sts. Work 3 (3, 1) row(s) even. Rep the last 4 (4, 2) rows 3 (3, 7) more times, then work the inc row once more—36 (52, 73) sts; piece meas about 3¼" (8.5 cm) from CO. Work even in stripe patt until piece meas 4½ (6, 9)" (11.5 [15, 23] cm) from CO, or 3½ (6, 8)" (9 [15, 20.5] cm) less than desired length from collar to base of tail, ending with a WS row. The standard length from collar to base of tail for this pattern is 8 (12, 17)" (20.5 [30.5, 43] cm). Beg with the next RS row, make a two-row buttonhole for bellyband, as given above. Work even in stripe patt until 1½ (2, 2½)" (3.8 [5, 6.5] cm) above previous buttonhole, ending with a WS row. Work another buttonhole the same as the first. Work even in stripe patt until piece meas 6¾ (9, 12½)" (17 [23, 31.5] cm) from CO, or about 1¼ (3, 4½)" (3.2 [7.5, 11.5] cm) less than desired length from base of tail to collar, ending with a WS row.

Shape Midsection:

K1f&b at each end of next 2 rows, then each end of every other row 3 (8, 11) times—46 (72, 99) sts. Work even in stripe patt, if necessary, until piece meas about *15"* 8 (12, 17)" (20.5 [30.5, 43] cm) from CO, ending with a WS row.

Shape Neck:

Knit across 18 (30, 42) sts, join a second ball of yarn, BO center 10 (12, 15) sts, knit to end—18 (30, 42) sts at each side. Working each side separately and joining more balls of yarn as needed to cont stripe patt in both sections, dec 1 st at each neck edge every row 8 (0, 10) times, then dec 1 st at each neck edge every other row 0 (12, 11) times—10 (18, 21) sts at each side. Work even in stripe patt, if necessary, until piece meas 1¼ (3¾, 5)" (3.2 [9.5, 12.5] cm) above center neck BO, about 9¼

Whichever color you choose as your trim will dominate and influence the play of color in your finished garment. Try out different colors of trim on your gauge swatch to see which one your like best before applying the final trim to your jacket.

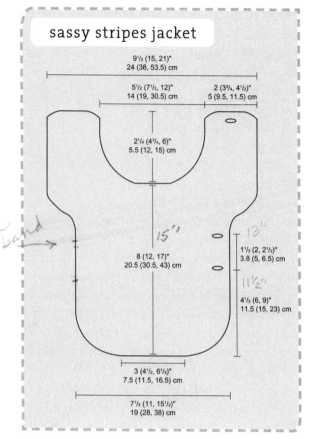

You can also knit your bellyband in seed stitch to play up the seed stitch texture that is part of the Sassy Stripes pattern.

(15¾, 22)" (23.5 [40, 56] cm) from CO, or desired length, ending with a WS row. Beg with the next RS row, make a two-row buttonhole on the right collar extension (the first section you come to on the RS) as foll: Work 4 (8, 10) sts in patt, BO the next 2 sts, work 4 (8, 9) sts in patt. On the next row, CO 2 sts over gap in previous row to complete buttonhole. Working each side separately, dec 1 st at each end of each collar extension on the next 2 rows—6 (14, 17) sts. BO all sts loosely.

edge trim

With RS facing, using crochet hook and color of your choice (C1 shown here), work a row of single crochet all around the outer edge of the jacket. Cut yarn and fasten off last st.

bellyband

Try the jacket on your dog and measure the desired length for the bellyband. Depending on the dog's size, knit the bellyband longer or shorter as needed to wrap comfortably around the rib cage, plus 1" (2.5 cm) for the buttonhole overlap. The standard bellyband for this pattern is 8 (12, 17)" (20.5 [30.5, 43] cm) long and 2½ (3, 3½)" (6.5 [7.5, 9] cm) wide.

Fold the jacket in half down the vertical centerline. On the left side of jacket (the side without buttonholes), mark positions matching buttonholes using safety pins or scrap yarn. Place another set of markers outside the first set, each ½" (1.3 cm) away from the first set of markers; the second set of markers should be about 2½ (3, 3½)" (6.5 [7.5, 9] cm) apart. With WS facing and color of your choice (C2 shown here), using crochet hook to assist if desired, pick up 12 (14, 17) sts along the jacket selvedge between the outer markers. Work in St st until bellyband meas 8 (12, 17)" (20.5 [30.5, 43] cm) from pickup row, or desired length plus 1" (2.5 cm) overlap. Loosely BO all sts.

finishing

Weave in all ends on WS. Sew buttons in place on bellyband and collar extension, wherever the best fit is achieved. Please attach your buttons very securely to prevent your dog from swallowing them.

funky felted jacket with saddlebags

FELTED DOG JACKET

making felt from a piece of knitting is easy. You knit the piece at a looser-than-normal gauge, larger than you want it to be, then throw it in the washing machine to shrink. Watch out—felting is addictive and you may get hooked! This multicolored felted jacket is perfect for a walk on a rainy day. It is warm, water resistant, and easy to care for. Consider making the coordinating button-on felted saddlebags and have your dog pull his or her own weight by carrying plastic bags, keys, or change for the paper.

FINISHED SIZE
Small (medium, large); shown in size medium.

FINISHED MEASUREMENTS
Before Felting
Length from collar to base of tail: 12 (18, 25½)"; 30.5 (45.5, 65) cm

Rib cage circumference (buttoned): 20½ (30¾, 44)"; 52 (78, 112) cm

After Felting
Length from collar to base of tail: 8 (12, 17)"; 20.5 (30.5, 43) cm

Rib cage circumference (buttoned): 14½ (22, 31½)"; 37 (56, 80) cm

MATERIALS
Yarn: 115 (225, 375) yards (105 [205, 345] meters) bulky weight *non*-machine-washable wool that knits to correct gauge in main color (MC); 20 (35, 60) yards (18 [32, 55] meters) of similar yarn in contrasting color (CC) for jacket. 35 yards (32 meters) CC and small amount of MC for one saddlebag.

Shown in Crystal Palace Labrador (100% wool; 90 yards [82 meters]/100 grams), #7166 ocean (blue/green/purple mix, MC) and #2801 purple (CC).

Needles: Size US 13 (9 mm) straight needles, or size to obtain gauge.

Notions: Three ¾" (1.9-cm) buttons for jacket, three ¾" (1.9-cm) buttons for each saddlebag, measuring tape, yarn needle, sharp-pointed yarn needle, scissors, safety pins, crochet hook size M/13 (9 mm), embroidery floss or thin cotton yarn to match main color.

Gauge: 9 sts and 12 rows = 4" (10 cm) in stockinette stitch (St st). Check your gauge before you begin. Note about gauge: You will want your prefelted knitting to be loose but not netlike. If you are trying out different yarns, be patient and flexible, and record your results for the future.

special techniques
make 1 (*m1*)
With the tip of the LH needle inserted from front to back, pick up the connecting strand between the two needles and place it on the LH needle. Knit the lifted strand through its back loop, twisting it to avoid leaving a hole.

two-row buttonhole for bellyband (worked over two rows)
Row 1: (RS) K2, BO 2 sts, knit to end of row.

Row 2: (WS) Purl to the gap created by the BO sts in the previous row, loosely CO 2 sts (the same number you bound off) over the gap, purl to end of row.

jacket
With MC loosely CO 8 (9, 10) sts. Work in St st, inc 2 sts in first row (RS) as foll: K2, M1, k4, M1, k4 (5, 6)— 10 (11, 12) sts. Inc 1 st at each end every row in this manner 6 (10, 16) more times—22 (31, 44) sts; piece meas about 2½ (3¾, 5¾)" (6.5 [9.5, 14.5] cm) from CO. Work even in St st until piece meas 6¾ (9, 13½)" (17 [23, 34.5] cm) from CO, or 5¼ (9, 12)" (13.5 [23, 30.5] cm) less than desired prefelted length from collar to base of tail, ending with a WS row. The standard prefelted length from collar to base of tail for this pattern is 12 (18, 25½)" (30.5 [45.5, 65] cm). Beg with the next RS row, make a two-row buttonhole for belly-

To make felt from knitting, you must use a 100% animal fiber yarn *that has not been treated to be machine-washable*. Each yarn will felt a little differently, so ask your local yarn shop to recommend good felting yarns. Keep in mind that felting is not an exact science and results will vary. The garment will lose approximately 33% in length and 20% in width after felting. Therefore the knitted dimensions should be about 1½ times as long (because you're going to lose about one-third the length in felting), and 1¼ times as wide (because you're going to lose about one-fifth the width in felting).

If you are trying a substitute yarn, choose one that will knit to the gauge given in this pattern. You can make a large test swatch at least 5" (12.5 cm) square and felt it in the washing machine. Record the gauge and dimensions of the swatch both before and after felting, and compare these percentages to those stated above. This will tell you how much longer and wider you have to make your prefelted pieces in order to achieve the correct size garment. However, the project itself is so quick to knit that, if you are the experimental type, you could treat the jacket as the swatch itself. Just remember to be flexible and open-minded about the results and finished dimensions if you choose to experiment. For further reading about felting, please see the Sources and Further Reading on page 111.

band, as given on page 85. Work even until 2¼ (3, 3¾)" (5.5 [7.5, 9.5] cm) above previous buttonhole, ending with a WS row. Work another buttonhole the same as the first. Work even until piece meas 10 (13½, 18¾)" (25.5 [34.5, 47.5] cm) from CO, or about 2 (4½, 6¾)" (5 [11.5, 17] cm) less than desired prefelted length from base of tail to collar, ending with a WS row.

Shape Midsection:
Inc as above at each end of next RS row, then every 4 (2, 2) rows 1 (5, 7) more time(s)—26 (43, 60) sts.

Work even in St st, if necessary, until piece meas about 12 (18, 25½)" (30.5 [45.5, 65] cm) from CO, ending with a WS row.

Shape Neck:
Knit across 9 (17, 25) sts, join a second ball of yarn, BO center 8 (9, 10) sts, knit to end—9 (17, 25) sts at each side. Working each side separately, dec 1 st at each neck edge every other row 2 (4, 12) times, then dec 1 st at each neck edge every 4 rows 1 (2, 0) time(s)—6 (11, 13) sts at each side. Work even in St st,

if necessary, until piece meas 2½ (6¼, 8)" (6.5 [16, 20.5] cm) above center neck BO, about 14½ (24¼, 33½)" (37 [61.5, 85] cm) from CO, or desired length, ending with a WS row. Beg with the next RS row, make a two-row buttonhole on the right collar extension (the first section you come to on the RS) as foll: K2 (5, 6), BO the next 2 sts, k2 (4, 5). On the next row, CO 2 sts over gap in previous row to complete buttonhole. Working each side separately, dec 1 st at each end of each collar extension on the next 2 rows—2 (7, 9) sts. BO all sts loosely. Weave in ends securely on WS.

bellyband

Depending on the size of your dog, the bellyband can be made longer or shorter as needed to wrap comfortably around the rib cage, plus 1" (2.5 cm) for button overlap. If in doubt of the length, make a longer band, and cut it to the correct size after felting and before applying the blanket stitch edging. The standard before-felting bellyband for this pattern is 12 (18, 25½)" (20.5 [45.5, 65] cm) long and 3¼ (3¾, 4½)" (8.5 [9.5, 11.5] cm) wide.

With CC, loosely CO 7 (8, 10) sts. Work in St st until bellyband meas 12 (18, 25½)" (30.5 [45.5, 65] cm) from CO, or desired length plus 1¼ inches (3.2 cm) before felting for overlap. Loosely BO all sts. Weave in ends securely on WS.

felting

When it's time to felt your items, the more the merrier. So if you want to make the felted saddlebags for this jacket, consider getting them all knit up to felt at the same time. The more friction available in the machine,

the faster and more efficient your felting will be. Consider placing large heavy things like old jeans in with your felting, but bear in mind that colors can bleed and yarns can shed fibers, so don't put anything that you love in with the felting load.

Place the items to be felted in a mesh lingerie bag or pillowcase that you can knot or tie shut. Set your machine to its lowest water level and the hottest water setting. Add a small amount of mild soap or detergent. If you use a no-rinse yarn wash product (available at most local yarn shops) you will not have to rinse suds out of your piece once it has been felted. Start the machine for a regular cycle, but don't leave! Stop the machine and pull out your pieces every five minutes at first, then every three minutes or so once you start to see results. Once felting begins, it tends to happen very quickly, so stay close!

Your target after-felting measurements for this project are shown on the diagram on page 88. When you think some or all of the items may be finished felting, take the pieces out of the bag, lightly blot the excess water with a towel, and take a quick measurement of the length and width to gauge your progress. If you check frequently, you can stay in control of the process. Remember, different yarns and different-sized objects felt at different rates.

As each piece is finished, remove it from the machine. Gently squeeze out excess water and lay the pieces flat to dry. Although you probably won't be able to regain any width lost, you can gently tug on your pieces to shape them to approximate the correct finished measurements, *gently* being the operative word here! Try to get your pieces as flat as possible before they dry. Felted knitting tends to have slightly uneven

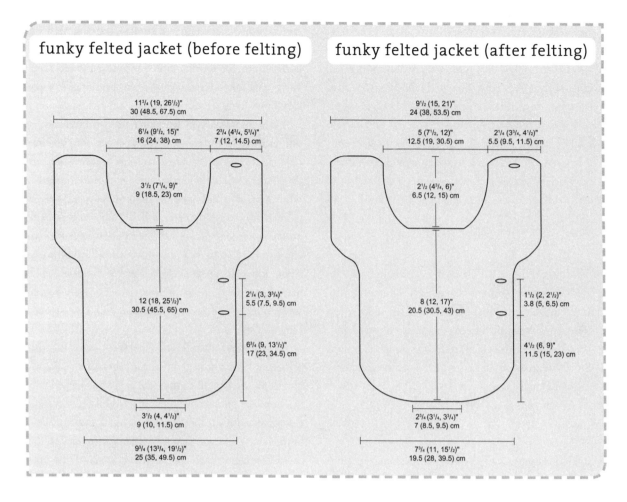

funky felted jacket (before felting)

11³/₄ (19, 26¹/₂)"
30 (48.5, 67.5) cm

6¹/₄ (9¹/₂, 15)"
16 (24, 38) cm

2³/₄ (4³/₄, 5³/₄)"
7 (12, 14.5) cm

3¹/₂ (7¹/₄, 9)"
9 (18.5, 23) cm

12 (18, 25¹/₂)"
30.5 (45.5, 65) cm

2¹/₄ (3, 3³/₄)"
5.5 (7.5, 9.5) cm

6³/₄ (9, 13¹/₂)"
17 (23, 34.5) cm

3¹/₂ (4, 4¹/₂)"
9 (10, 11.5) cm

9³/₄ (13³/₄, 19¹/₂)"
25 (35, 49.5) cm

funky felted jacket (after felting)

9¹/₂ (15, 21)"
24 (38, 53.5) cm

5 (7¹/₂, 12)"
12.5 (19, 30.5) cm

2¹/₄ (3³/₄, 4¹/₂)"
5.5 (9.5, 11.5) cm

2¹/₂ (4³/₄, 6)"
6.5 (12, 15) cm

8 (12, 17)"
20.5 (30.5, 43) cm

1¹/₂ (2, 2¹/₂)"
3.8 (5, 6.5) cm

4¹/₂ (6, 9)"
11.5 (15, 23) cm

2³/₄ (3¹/₄, 3³/₄)"
7 (8.5, 9.5) cm

7³/₄ (11, 15¹/₂)"
19.5 (28, 39.5) cm

edges. You can further flatten them once they're dry with a steam iron, or when applying the edge trim.

edge trim

After the jacket is felted and dry, cut a length of MC about 18" (45.5 cm) long and thread it on a sharp-pointed yarn needle. With RS facing, beg at bottom left edge, work blanket stitch embroidery evenly around the entire edge of jacket. Join new lengths of yarn as needed, and securely and invisibly weaving in the ends on the WS of the felted piece as you go. If you want to coax a wavy edge into being flatter, space your blanket stitches closer together in the wavy section. Try the jacket on the dog, and pin the bellyband temporarily in place with safety pins. Cut bellyband to the correct length, if necessary, allowing for 1" (2.5 cm) of over-

Think about working the blanket stitch edging in a contrasting color, or a different textured yarn.

lap. Work blanket stitch embroidery around sides of bellyband in the same manner as the jacket.

finishing

Fold the jacket in half vertically, and mark positions for two buttons opposite buttonholes. Center the bellyband over the markers on the WS of jacket. With matching embroidery floss or thin cotton yarn, securely sew bellyband in place on WS. Sew buttons in place on bellyband and collar extension, wherever the best fit is achieved. Please attach your buttons very securely to prevent your dog from swallowing them.

- - - - - - - - - - - - - - - - saddlebags - - - - - - - - - - - - - - - -

if you are hooked on felting, or if you want to start with something simple, try this little project. These tiny bags have buttonholes on the back, so depending on the day and his or her mood, your pet can wear them or not.

FINISHED MEASUREMENTS

Before Felting

About 5¼" (13.5 cm) wide and 6" (15 cm) high, assembled with flap closed

After Felting

About 4" (10 cm) square, assembled with flap closed

saddlebags

See materials, gauge, special techniques, and felting instructions for the Funky Felted Dog Jacket on page 84.

With CC, loosely CO 12 sts. Work even in St st until piece meas 10¾" (27.5 cm) from CO. On the next row, make 2 buttonholes as foll: Work 2 sts, BO 2 sts, work 4 sts, BO 2 sts, work to end of row. On the next row, CO 2 sts above each gap in the previous row to complete buttonholes. Work even until piece meas 12" (30.5 cm) from CO. Shape flap: Dec 1 st at each end on the next

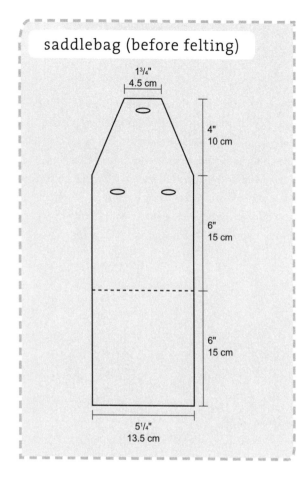

saddlebag (before felting)

1¾"
4.5 cm

4"
10 cm

6"
15 cm

6"
15 cm

5¼"
13.5 cm

aligned with first row of flap shaping. With CC yarn threaded on yarn needle, loosely sew side seams, leaving flap free. Weave in all ends securely on WS.

felting

Follow felting instructions for Funky Felted Jacket on page 87.

edge trim

After the saddlebag is felted and dry, cut a length of MC about 18" (45.5 cm) long and thread it on a sharp-pointed yarn needle. Beg at the top of one side seam, work blanket stitch embroidery evenly around the triangular flap and straight across the opening at the top. Join new lengths of yarn as needed, and securely and invisibly weaving in the ends on the WS of the felted piece as you go. If you want to coax a wavy edge into being flatter, space your blanket stitches closer together in the wavy section.

finishing

Sew one button to front of bag to correspond with buttonhole on the flap. Temporarily pin the saddlebag to the dog jacket, locating it in your preferred spot. For the jacket shown, the saddlebag is centered above the bellyband, with the bottom edge of the bag just above the edge of the jacket.

Mark positions for two buttons on the jacket to correspond to the buttonholes of the bag. Sew buttons in place at marked positions on jacket. Please attach your buttons very securely to prevent your dog from swallowing them. Button saddlebag to jacket.

row—10 sts. Work 3 rows even. Rep the last 4 rows once, then work dec row once more—6 sts; piece meas about 13½" (34.5 cm) from CO. On the next row, make a single buttonhole as foll: Work 2 sts, BO 2 sts, work 2 sts. On the next row, CO 2 sts above gap in previous row to complete buttonhole. On the next row, dec 1 st at each side—4 sts. BO all sts loosely. Fold bag along dotted line shown on diagram so cast-on edge is

toy bone

FELTED DOG TOY

this little toy will make a great stocking stuffer or "just because" present for your four-legged friend. Fill it with wool or cedar chips. There are two sizes, large and small, so you can knit the perfect size for your favorite pup. Shown here in a mohair/wool blend (small bone) and 100% wool (large bone), these toys knit up fast in garter stitch on big needles.

Please read the information about felting and choosing a yarn for felting in the instructions for the Funky Felted Jacket with Saddlebags on page 84.

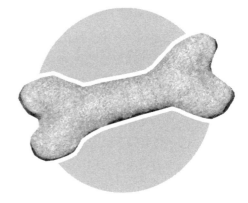

FINISHED MEASUREMENTS
Before Felting
About 5½ (7½)" (14 [19] cm) wide and 12½ (15)" (31.5 [38] cm) long
After Felting
About 4½ (6)" (11.5 [15] cm) wide and 8½ (11)" (21.5 [28] cm) long

MATERIALS
Yarn: 100 (175) yards (90 [160] meters) Aran weight *non-superwash* wool that knits to correct gauge.
Small bone shown in Dale of Norway Tiur (60% mohair, 40% wool; 126 yards [115 meters]/50 grams), #8533 light green. Large bone shown in Crystal Palace Tekapo (100% wool; 218 yards [199 meters]/100 grams), #04 natural white.
Needles: Size US 10 (6 mm) straight needles, or size to obtain gauge.
Size US 10 (6 mm) set of four double-pointed needles (dpn) suggested for portability and to use as stitch holders.
Notions: Measuring tape, yarn needle, scissors, stitch holders or scrap yarn (optional if using dpn), cedar chips or wool fiber for stuffing.
Gauge: 16 sts and 24 rows = 4" (10 cm) in garter stitch, before felting.

note

Small bone directions are given first, with large bone directions in parentheses. If only one number is given it applies to both bones.

bone (make 2)

First end: Loosely CO 3 (5) sts. Work in garter st (knit all sts every row), and on the next 2 rows, inc 1 st at each end of row—7 (9) sts. Work 2 rows even. Inc 1 st each end of every 4th row 1 (2) time(s)—9 (13) sts. You have now completed one half of the first end of the bone. Cut yarn and place these sts on a stitch holder or length of scrap yarn, or leave on dpn. Work a second half the same as the first, but leave sts on the needle.

Center Section:

Knit across the live sts on the needle, CO 2 (3) sts, return held sts to needles, and knit to end—20 (29) sts.

Inc 1 st at each end of next row—22 (31) sts. Work even for 20 (24) rows. On the next row, dec 1 st at each end—20 (29) sts. Work 3 rows even. Rep the last 4 rows one more time, then work dec row once more—

Think about adding special embellishments to customize: a ribbon or bows (securely attached so your dog doesn't swallow them), or embroider your dog's name on the bone *after* felting.

16 (25) sts. Inc 1 st at each end every other row three times—22 (31) sts. Work even for 20 (24) rows. On the next row, dec 1 st at each end of row—20 (29) sts.

Second End:
Knit across 9 (13) sts, join second ball of yarn, BO center 2 (3) sts, knit to end—9 (13) sts at each side. Working each side separately, cont as foll: Dec 1 st at each end of next row, then work 3 rows even—7 (11) sts at each side. For the large bone *only,* rep the last 4 rows once more—7 (9) sts at each side. Dec 1 st at each end every other row two times—3 (5) sts at each side. Loosely BO all sts. Make a second bone the same as the first.

finishing

Weave in all ends and close up any holes. With yarn threaded on yarn needle, sew the 2 pieces together loosely, leaving a 2" to 3" (5- to 7.5-cm) opening in one long side for stuffing later. Felt according to the directions for the Funky Felted Jacket on page 84. Using the stopper end of a knitting needle or the eraser end of a pencil to pack stuffing into corners, fill with the stuffing of your choice, such as cedar chips (available at pet and natural-food stores), or wool fiber (available from craft stores that carry spinning supplies). Carefully and securely sew the opening closed with matching yarn.

Learn about the different felting properties of various yarns by trying this project in different fibers and colors—maybe even stripes! Word to the wise: Dyed yarns felt more rapidly and completely than un-dyed or light colors.

knitting pretty

So much thought and care has gone into the creation of your knitted gift. You've carefully selected the pattern and the materials and have created a one-of-a-kind item. Now that it's time to give your gift to the lucky recipient, shouldn't its presentation be one-of-a-kind too?

When I am making a gift project, I like the presentation to be as much a part of the process as the knitting itself. I think about the person I'm giving my gift to—does this person have a penchant for purple? Is he or she an earthy, organic type? Does this particular critter have a yen for doggy treats? Is this pup chic or macho? Then I decide how I can incorporate these endearing qualities into the way I present this special gift.

Here are a few ideas for creative, unique, and thematic gift presentations.

for babes

- Present your knitted item in a gift basket shaped like a baby carriage (available at most major craft/basket stores)
- Go *au naturel*—Wrap your gift in brown kraft paper and tie it with natural twill ribbon; top with an unpainted wooden rattle
- Wrap your gift in a functional cloth, such as a receiving blanket, or crib sheets
- Use the "old-is-new" approach—wrap your gift in vintage cloth or fabric
- Accompany a simple knit with thematic baby products—bath, bedding, stroller items
- Use a functional item as packaging—a beautiful diaper bag, a Moses basket, or a bassinet
- Group Gift—Arrange for your knitting group to fill up a beautiful diaper bag or gift basket with custom-made handknits

for pups

- Tie dog treats or toys (perhaps the felted bones in this collection?) on your gift
- Put your knitted gift inside a dog biscuit box or a reusable treat tin
- Present your gift fetch-ingly wrapped in doggy-themed fabric
- Give your knitted gift with other helpful doggy items—a groovy collar, a set of matching shoes . . .
- Place your knitted gifts in a soft dog bed to surely earn canine love!

k1, p2

KNITTING TERMS AND ABBREVIATIONS

BEG	beginning
BO	bind off
CC	contrast color
CIRC	circular, as in circular needle
CM	centimeter
CO	cast on
CONT	continue
DEC	decrease(s), decreasing
DPN	double-pointed needle(s)
EOR	every other row
FOLL	follows, following
GARTER ST	garter stitch: knit all sts every row

GAUGE	The number of stitches across and/or vertical rows in a specified number of inches. Matching the gauge required by the pattern is essential to knitting a project in the correct size.
IN	inch
INC	increase(s), increasing
K	knit
K1, P1 RIB	knit one, purl one rib: *k1, p1; rep from *, ending k1 for an odd number of sts
K1F&B	knit into front and back of same st to inc 1 st
K2TOG	knit 2 stitches together as one (a type of decrease)
LH	left hand
MC	main color
MEAS	measure(s)
NDL(S)	needle(s)
P	purl
PSSO	pass slipped stitch over
PATT	pattern
REM	remain(s), remaining
REP	repeat(s)
REV ST ST	reverse stockinette stitch: purl all sts on RS, knit all sts on WS
RH	right hand
RS	right side (the "public" or outside of the knitting)
SL	slip

SSK	slip, slip, knit: slip 2 sts to RH needle as if to knit, return them to the LG needle, and knit them together through their back loops (a type of decrease)
ST ST	stockinette stitch: knit all sts on RS, purl all sts on WS
ST(S)	stitch(es)
TOG	together
WS	wrong side (the "private" or inside of the knitting)
WYIF	with yarn in front
YO	yarnover

needles have them

blocking

Knitted fabric is blocked to even out any irregular stitches and to flatten curling edges. This can be done using a steam iron on cool setting, or by washing a garment, patting it into the desired shape and allowing it to dry flat. Cables and textured pattern stitches should be blocked *only if absolutely necessary*, as blocking can flatten stitchwork and compromise the desired effect.

buttonholes

While you are knitting a piece, you can place holes or breaks in the fabric to accommodate button closures. There are two methods of making buttonholes used in this collection: the two-row buttonhole and the yarnover buttonhole. Both are easy to do. The two-row buttonhole gives a more finished look and is completed in two steps. The yarnover buttonhole makes a hole in the fabric and is completed simply in one step. Details for buttonhole placement can be found in the individual patterns, but the conventional location for buttonholes is on the right front (as if you were wearing the sweater) for girls' cardigans, and on the left front for boys' or unisex garments.

Intuitively Placed Buttonholes

First, knit the front piece that will not have buttonholes. Then, before you work the other side, mark the button locations on the first front with contrasting yarn or safety pins. Do this by either measuring or "eyeballing." When you make the front that has buttonholes, as you knit, compare it against the front with the marked button positions. When you reach the approximate location of each marker, it's time to make a buttonhole. Continue in this manner until all the buttonholes have been completed.

Yarnover Buttonhole

Knit to the desired location of the buttonhole, k2tog, yo, work to end of row.

Two-Row Buttonhole (worked over two rows)

Row 1: Work as established to desired location of buttonhole, BO 1 or 2 sts as directed, work to end of row.
Row 2: Work as established to the gap created by the BO sts in the previous row, loosely CO 1 or 2 sts (the same number you bound off) over the gap, work to end of row.

casting on

Casting on is the technique of putting stitches on the needles to begin knitting a piece of fabric. There are many methods of casting on, each giving a unique quality to the edge finish. Here are two: a method called knitting-on, which is used for shaping the dog jackets in this collection, and my favorite cast-on method, the two-tail or long-tail cast on. Please refer to a knitting reference book for more information and detailed instructions on the various types of cast ons.

Knitting-On

This method of cast on is made by knitting a new stitch, and instead of leaving the new stitch on the right hand (RH) needle and letting the old stitch drop from the left hand (LH) needle, the old stitch stays on the LH needle, and the new stitch is passed back to the LH needle next to its "parent." To work this cast on, insert the RH needle into the first stitch on the LH needle as if to knit, then wrap the yarn and pull through a new loop as if forming a knit stitch, but do not slip the old stitch from the LH needle. Pass the new loop you have just made from the RH needle to the LH needle. To make the next new stitch, knit into the stitch just made, which is now first on the LH needle, and repeat as needed.

Two-Tail or Long-Tail Cast On

This method gives a sturdy and neat edge to your work. If you do not know how to work this cast on, please refer to an illustrated knitting reference for directions. Here are some of my tips for using this method successfully. When deciding how long a tail to leave, a good rule of thumb is to allow approximately 1 inch for each stitch you plan to cast on, then make your starting slipknot that distance or more from the cut end of the yarn. When you place the slipknot on the needle, it should be loose enough to slide back and forth but snug enough so that it doesn't slide off the needle if you shake it.

circular needles and circular knitting

Circular needles are two short needles joined by a plastic cord or cable. The needles themselves may be made of aluminum, plastic, wood, or bamboo. Circular needles are commonly available in 16", 24", and 29" lengths, although other lengths are made, too. If you are using them to knit in the round (see below), choose a needle with a length slightly smaller than the circumference of your work so the stitches will not be stretched tightly around the circle.

The main purpose of circular needles is to allow for knitting in the round, which creates a knitted tube. This is done by casting on the required number of stitches, carefully bringing the two ends of the cast-on stitches together to form a circle, and knitting around and around. When knitting circularly, or "in the round," the right side or "outside" of the knitted fabric is always facing you.

knitting flat on circular needles

Circular needles are very helpful if you want to knit a large piece of fabric back and forth. This may seem odd at first, but is an efficient and ergonomic way of knitting. To knit flat using circular needles, cast on the number of stitches given in your pattern onto one end of the needle, and ignore the other end—let it flap around while you complete your cast on. Then begin knitting, pretending that the two needles are not connected. Work across the row, and then turn your work over, just as you would if you were using straight needles. Again, pretending the two needles are not connected, begin the next row. As the knitting grows, most of the fabric will hang from the connecting cable between the needles and rest in your lap, rather than hanging from the ends of straight needles. It requires much less work for your wrists and shoulders to support the knitting this way. Additionally, knitting flat on circular needles allows you to knit across a very wide piece of fabric, such as the back of an extra-large sweater or the width of a blanket—

items that simply will not fit onto the longest of straight needles.

decreasing

Decreasing is a method for reducing the number of stitches on your needle, and is also a technique for manipulating the shape of a knitted piece, such as making a neck opening rounded or a sleeve narrower at the cuff. The most straightforward and common method of decreasing is to knit (or purl) two stitches together as if they are one. The abbreviation for this is k2tog (or p2tog). To work two stitches together, insert the tip of the RH needle into the first two sts on the left needle, pretending they are one stitch. Then wrap the yarn as usual, and pull a new loop through the two old sts, letting them both fall from the LH needle. Unless otherwise noted, use this method of decreasing for all the projects in this book.

double-pointed needles

Double-pointed needles (dpn's) are short needles with points on both ends that usually come in sets of four or five. They are used for knitting small-diameter circles, or to continue "knitting in the round" (see "Circular Needles and Circular Knitting") when the circumference of your work is too small for a circular needle. American patterns typically call for four dpn's—three to hold the stitches of the work in progress, and the fourth needle to knit.

It is much easier to get the hang of dpn's if you introduce them into work that has already been started, such as the decrease rounds at the top of a hat. When it is time to switch over to dpn's, take one of your dpn's and begin knitting around in the established pattern. Work approximately one-third of the stitches, then let go of the first dpn. The tension of the stitches will keep it in place. It seems awkward at first, but don't worry. Now, pick up the second dpn and work the next third of the stitches. Drop that needle, pick up your third dpn, and finish the round. When you have worked all the stitches from your circular needle, it will be empty and you can simply set it aside. Now, using the fourth dpn, continue working around the circle of stitches. As you empty each left needle, switch it to your right hand and it will become your new working needle.

One thing you will notice about working with dpn's is that you cannot use a marker between the first and last stitches of the round, as you could with a circular needle, because the marker will fall off the end of the dpn. If you can still see it, the position of your cast-on tail will let you know when you have finished a round. If not, place a removable stitch marker or safety pin in your fabric to indicate the beginning of each round, moving the marker up as your work progresses.

finishing

Finishing is made up of the steps and techniques needed to complete a knitting project, and includes things such as blocking, sewing seams, weaving in ends, adding neck finishing and edge treatments, and sewing on buttons.

I've noticed that finishing is usually a "love it or hate it" kind of thing. Many knitters want the sweater or project to be done when the knitting is done, and don't realize that the final touches may, in some cases, take almost as long as the knitting itself. Resist the urge to skimp on finishing. You put a lot of yourself into the project in addition to time and money. Focus your intention on being thorough and proper, and enjoy the details of making your creation as magnificent as it can be. It is good discipline to see the project through to the end with as much purposefulness as you put into it when you started.

If you are one of the many knitters who just hate finishing, consider seeking out an individual who does professional finishing—often found through your local yarn shop. Be prepared to pay a sizable fee for this service, but if you hate to finish because you find it tedious and time-consuming, you may well appreciate why finishers charge as much as they do. If you want to improve your finishing skills, and perhaps find the joy in the fine points of the process, see if your local yarn shop or knitting guild offers classes in finishing.

gauge

Gauge is the number of stitches and rows in a specified number of inches or centimeters that the designer used for a particular project. You must match the gauge given in the pattern or your knitted pieces will not measure the same dimensions as intended, and your sweater or project will not turn out the correct size. Nothing is more heartbreaking than completing a project early in your knitting career to find that it does not fit or hangs all wrong because you did not take time to properly check your gauge. Gauge can also affect how much yarn you use. If you have more stitches and rows per measuring unit than called for, the project will use more yarn, and you might run short.

Before you begin any project, knit a gauge swatch,

or a small sample piece of knitting, usually about 4–5" (10–12.5 cm) square. This will give you the opportunity both to check the size of your stitches and to practice any pattern stitches used in the project. Most directions give a gauge in terms of a 4" (10-cm) square. Start with the needle size recommended for your project, but bear in mind that this is only a *recommended* needle size and should be considered a starting point.

When you cast on for your swatch, cast on at least 4 more stitches than the number you want to measure. In other words, if your desired gauge is measured over 20 stitches, cast on 24, and work in the stitch pattern given for more than 4" in length. This is helpful for two reasons. First, the bigger your swatch, the more accurately it can be measured. Second, it is best to measure gauge over the center of the fabric, and not too close to the selvedges, the cast-on edge, or the needles. The stitches in these areas are not representative of the main part of the knitting, and can give you false results if you include them when checking your gauge. If you simply cast on 20 stitches and check to see if they measure 4" (10 cm) across, you could be doing yourself and your project an injustice.

Use a tape measure, "Knit Check" tool, or ruler to count the number of stitches for the gauge. If you have fewer stitches in 4" (10 cm) than the pattern, then your stitches are slightly too large, so you should switch to a smaller needle. If you have more stitches in your swatch than the pattern, then your stitches are too small, and you should try a larger needle. Keep experimenting with your needle size as needed until you match the stitch and row count dead on. Remember, it won't take you any longer to knit your project on smaller needles if they're the right size required for you to get the correct gauge!

increasing

This is the term for adding a new stitch or stitches to your needle. Unlike casting on, where you place a group of new stitches on the needle, an increase adds only one stitch at a time in a specific place for a specific purpose. Increasing is used to manipulate the shape of a knitted piece, such as making the sides of a piece curve, or to widen a sleeve that is knit from the cuff upward.

There are several methods for increasing, and two of the more commonly used increases are featured in this collection. The make one method is a clean way to introduce a new stitch into a row without creating a hole or bar. Knitting in the front and back of the same stitch is an easy way to add a stitch at the beginning and/or end of a row.

Make one (M1)

With the tip of the LH needle inserted from front to back, pick up the connecting strand between the two needles and place it on the LH needle. Knit the lifted strand through its back loop, twisting it to avoid leaving a hole.

Knit into the Front and Back of the Same Stitch (K1f&b)

Work the stitch to be increased in the usual manner, but do not remove the old stitch from the LH needle. Instead, insert the RH needle into the back of the same stitch and knit it again. Then remove the old stitch from the LH needle, and you will have two stitches from one stitch.

intarsia

Intarsia is a technique for knitting blocks of color using a separate strand of yarn for each block. Rather than having the strands attached to lots of different balls of yarn, each strand is either wound onto a bobbin or, if the color sections are small, simply left hanging at the back of your work until it is needed again. Unlike stranded knitting, where unused colors are carried all the way across the back of the work from edge to edge (such as you would see in a Nordic-style sweater), intarsia blocks are worked without carrying yarns behind the work. The yarn for each color section is used only for the "island" of stitches in each color area and kept to the confines of its particular color block. When working an intarsia block, it is important to twist the yarns together at the color change (as if locking elbows). This prevents a slit or hole from forming in your fabric at the change. For more information on intarsia and color knitting in general, please consult a well-illustrated knitting reference book.

novelty yarns

These are any yarns that are not smooth, regularly spun yarns. Some things that fall in the category of novelties are fur, confetti, "eyelash," metallic, or heavily textured yarns. Novelty yarns are popular to use for accessories such as scarves, as trim for a garment knitted in a more traditional fiber, or as a carry-along yarn. This last method involves holding one strand of a conventional type of yarn together with a novelty yarn and working with them together as one yarn. Very interesting textural and color effects can be achieved this way, and the two yarns together will knit up to a bulkier gauge than just one of the yarns on its own. This is a fun way to customize a garment or play around with design ideas and yarns that may already be in your stash.

picking up stitches

When you are asked to pick up stitches, it is usually to create an edge finish or to knit a new part of the project, such as a sleeve, out from the edge of an existing piece. In the patterns given in this book, stitches for the sleeves are picked up at the armhole edge and knit down to the cuff, rather than knitting them separately and sewing them on later.

To help you to pick up stitches more neatly and evenly, consider using a crochet hook to help you. With the right side of the fabric facing you, find the location where you will begin picking up stitches. Lay a strand of yarn behind the fabric. Using the working end of the strand (the one attached to the yarn supply and not the short tail), insert the crochet hook through to the back of the fabric and pull up a loop from the yarn strand held behind. Transfer this loop to the RH needle. Repeat, continuing to work toward the ball, until you have the number of stitches you need.

Figuring out how close together your pickup stitches should be can be frustrating. To intuitively pick up stitches, note the total number of stitches you will need. Mentally divide this number by four, and visualize the pickup edge divided into four equal sections. For example, when picking up stitches for a sleeve, if you begin at the underarm, the shoulder seam will be at the halfway point. Therefore, when you are halfway to the shoulder seam you should have picked up about a quarter of the stitches needed. If you have to "fudge" and pick up a few extra stitches to make things work out correctly, place these extra pickups close to the underarm where they will be less noticeable. Because knitted fabric typically has more rows to the inch than stitches to the inch, try picking up one stitch per row for two rows, then skip a row; this will give you a pickup rate of about two stitches for every three rows. If it doesn't look right, you can easily pull out the picked-up stitches and try again. With each attempt you gain practice in picking up stitches neatly, and learn how to better judge where to place your pickups.

reading charts

Knitting charts are a universal visual language for knitting. They are read as if looking at the right or "public" side of knitted fabric. When knitting a flat piece back and forth, the charts are read back and forth, just like the construction of the fabric. Begin in the lower right corner on RS rows, and read from right to left. For WS rows, read from left to right. In this book, each row is numbered on the side of the chart where you begin that row. If you are knitting in the round with the RS always facing you, all rows are read from the right side from right to left. Charts are usually accompanied by keys that explain how to work each chart symbol. Sections of knitting to be repeated are typically indicated by a heavy or colored outline. Work any stitches before the marked repeat box once, then repeat the stitches inside the box the desired number of times, and finish by working any stitches after the repeat box once.

textured and cable knitting charts

Charts represent the right side of the knitted fabric. Therefore, a stitch purled on the wrong side will be shown as it appears on the right side, as a knit stitch. Each knitting chart is accompanied by a symbol key that will explain how to work each symbol on both right and wrong sides, if necessary. If you are working a project with cables, the symbol for each type of cable will be accompanied by directions on how to proceed. If you are working from a lace knitting chart, it will use symbols specific to the increases, decreases, and yarnover holes used to create the lace pattern. Usually, each grid square of a chart represents one stitch, and you should follow the row across, working the stitches indicated as you come to them at the location where the symbol is shown.

Although it might feel like learning a new language, becoming comfortable with using charts is a wonderful way to become a more intuitive knitter. Once you are familiar with them, the symbols actually look like the completed fabric. This visual language can liberate you from written instructions and long strings of abbreviations such as "P2, K6, P2, C4B, P2, C5F, LT," and other such maddening left brain fodder. You can begin to interact with your knitting so that you can literally "read" what to do next. Furthermore, the symbol language of knitting is an international language. Once you know the basic symbols, you can knit fun and truly exciting projects from many different foreign books or magazines.

color knitting charts

Charts showing patterns for multiple colors are read just like textured and cable charts, and they show the appearance of the knitting as seen from the right side. A symbol key will accompany the chart, explaining which color or symbol used in the chart represents which color. For two-color stitch patterns, a blank square will represent the main color background (abbreviated as MC), and a symbol or colored square will be used for the contrast color (CC). For projects that use more than one contrast color, they may be referred to as contrast color 1 (CC1), contrast color 2 (CC2), etc. The number of squares shown in a certain color indicates the number of stitches you are to work in that color. When you are carrying the unused color or colors behind your knitting until they are needed again, the process is called "stranding" or "stranded knitting." Always carry the unused strands loosely across the back of the work, or your tension will be affected and the knitting could pucker and lose elasticity. If you strand too tightly, stitches made with the tight yarn can sink into the surrounding color and may disappear entirely.

three-needle bind-off technique

The three-needle bind-off technique is used for joining the live stitches from two pieces of fabric to produce what looks like a perfect seam. It is especially useful for joining shoulders, as is done in many of the projects in this collection. It gets its name from the fact that it requires three needles, two to hold the live stitches of the pieces to be joined, and a third needle for working the bind off. The technique is very similar to that of a regular bind off.

Place the stitches to be joined on two needles, if they aren't already, and hold the pieces so that their right sides are touching and the tips of both needles point in the same direction. If you are joining a shoulder, check to make sure you are carefully matching the garment pieces properly—left shoulder to left shoulder and right to right. These two needles will be held parallel to each other in your left hand and will be treated as a single LH needle.

Holding a third needle in your right hand, insert the tip through the first stitch on both the front and back needles in your left hand. Knit the two stitches together as one, and slide them both off their respective needles. Repeat this once more; you now have a second stitch on the RH needle. Then perform the first bind off by passing the first stitch on the RH needle over the second stitch, just as for a regular bind off; there will be one stitch remaining on the RH needle. Repeat this process from the beginning, binding off one stitch as soon as you have two stitches on the RH needle, until all the stitches are bound off and the two pieces are perfectly joined, stitch for stitch. Cut the yarn, leaving a 6–10" (15–25.5 cm) tail, and draw the tail through the last stitch to fasten off. Weave in the end.

If you are having a hard time visualizing this process, have someone read it aloud to you while you give it a try. If you are still not getting it, please refer to a well-illustrated knitting reference book, or ask a knitting friend for a demonstration. This technique can also be referred to as "binding off two pieces together."

weaving in ends

This is a crucial part of finishing your work (see "Finishing"). Ends, just like knots, have a nasty little tendency to wiggle their way to the front of your work, especially if you have ends front and center, and it seems as if there are *always* ends to weave in at the front and center of a sweater!

To minimize the number of ends to weave in when you finish a garment, always try to join a new ball of yarn at the beginning of a row. If the yarn is getting close to the end, do not start a row unless the length of the remaining yarn is at least six times the width across the row—that will make sure that you have enough yarn left to make it all the way across.

To make weaving ends easier, try to leave yarn tails that are at least 8" (20.5 cm) long. When weaving in an end along a seam, thread the end through a yarn needle and sew up the same path as your seam for about 1" (2.5 cm). Then reverse direction and weave the end back along the same path for about 1" (2.5 cm). This secures the yarn very well, and allows you to cut the yarn flush with the surface of the fabric.

If you have to weave in an end in the middle of your knitted fabric, work the yarn into the back of a diagonal line of stitches, instead of straight across a row, or up and down a column of stitches, making sure the yarn you are weaving in is not visible from the right side. Then, reverse direction and trace the same path back to where you started. This, again, allows you to cut the end flush with the surface of the fabric. Working on the diagonal minimizes the amount of tugging the end will receive from side to side, making it more likely to stay put and not wiggle its way free.

increase!

SOURCES AND FURTHER READING

Darlington, Rohana. *Irish Knitting: Patterns Inspired by Ireland*. London: A&C Black, 1992.

Editors of Vogue Knitting. *Vogue Knitting: The Ultimate Knitting Book*. New York: Sixth and Spring Books, 2002.

Galeskas, Beverly. *Felted Knits*. Loveland, CO: Interweave Press, 2003.

Manning, Tara Jon. "Aran Hand Knitting—History, Design and Technique." Master's thesis, Colorado State University, 1997.

———. "Celtic Images and Family Patterns: Folklore of the Aran Sweater." *Interweave Knits*, vol. 2, no. 3 (fall 1997): 48.

Patons Yarn Company. *A Dog's Life,* Pattern leaflet. Listowel, ON: Patons, 2002.

Polley, Laura. *Pet Pleasers*. Pattern leaflet. Big Sandy, TX: Annie's Attic, 2002.

Schwartz, Judith. *Dogs in Knits*. Loveland, CO: Interweave Press, 2001.

Starmore, Alice. *Aran Knitting*. Loveland, CO: Interweave Press, 1997.

Vickrey, Anne Einset. *The Art of Feltmaking: Basic Techniques for Making Jewelry, Miniatures, Dolls, Buttons, Wearables, Puppets, Masks and Fine Art Pieces.* New York: Watson-Guptill Publications, 1997.

Walker, Barbara. *A Treasury of Knitting Patterns.* Pittsville, WI: Schoolhouse Press, 1998.

in the bag

MATERIALS AND RESOURCES

project kits and Tara's original design patterns are available from:

Tara Handknitting Designs
www.tarahandknitting.com
PO Box 573
Boulder, Colorado 80306-0573

many heartfelt thanks are extended to the manufacturers and distributors of the fine yarns and notions shown in this book:

Artful Yarns
Distributed by JCA, Inc.

Brown Sheep Yarn
100662 County Road 16
Mitchell, Nebraska 69357
800-826-9136
www.brownsheep.com

Cascade Yarns
1224 Andover Park E
Tukwila, Washington 98188
www.cascadeyarns.com

Crystal Palace Yarns
2320 Bissel Avenue
Redmond, California 94804
800-666-7455
www.straw.com

Dale of Norway USA
N16 W23390 Stoneridge Drive, Suite A
Waukesha, Wisconsin 53188
800-441-DALE
www.dale.no

JCA, Inc.
Distributor of Reynolds Yarn and Artful Yarns
35 Scales Lane
Townsend, Massachusetts 01469
800-225-6340

JHB International (supplier of buttons used in this book)
1955 South Quince Street
PO Box 22395
Denver, Colorado 80222
800-525-9007
www.buttons.com

Muench Yarns
285 Bel Marin Keys Blvd., Unit J
Novato, California 94949-5763
415-883-6375
www.muenchyarns.com

Mission Falls
Distributed in the United States by Unique Kolours
800-25-2DYE4
www.missionfalls.com

Reynolds Yarns
Distributed by JCA, Inc.

local yarn shops

Keep the local knitting community in your area flourishing by supporting your local yarn and crafts shops. These retailers are often the heart and hub of knitting groups, friendships, and support networks. To find a local yarn store in your area, please visit one of the Internet sites listed here, or run a search through your favorite Internet search engine for "your town" "yarn shop." Yarn shops come and go, so check your current phone book for up-to-date contact information.

Knitter's Magazine Shopfinder:
www.knittinguniverse.com/xrx/athena/shopfinder.php

Interweave Press Traveling Knitter's Sourcebook:
www.interweave.com/knit/sourcebook.asp.

WoolWorks: www.woolworks.org/stores.html

About.com Yarn Shops, Manufacturers, and Reviews: www.knitting.about.com
Type "local yarn shop" in search window.

who's who

 audrey Audrey is an Italian Greyhound. She lives in New York City. She wishes Starbucks would make a canine-friendly beverage.

 chou chou Chou Chou, a Yorkie, enjoys fashion. She can be found with her people at Zoomies, a dog boutique in lower Manhattan. Visit their website www.zoomiesnyc.com.

 ellie r. Ellie's favorite food is peas. She loves to climb stairs, and she lives in New Jersey.

gidget Gidget is a Brussels Griffon. She lives on the Upper East Side, but spends her days in an office in the garment district with her person. She loves to shop.

 hugh b. Hugh spends time in Ireland, France, and New York City. He has always had red hair; this is his first modeling assignment.

 luke Luke lives in New York City. His favorite treat is any meat or vegetable prepared for humans, especially Chinese snow peas.

 m'lee M'lee is a nine-year-old Shih Tzu. Her favorite treats are made by her person—you can buy them too at www.dogchewz.com. She lives in Manhattan.

 nora k. Nora lives in Brooklyn. She attends a co-ed knitting club every Tuesday night with her parents.

 oliver Oliver is a three-year-old Chihuahua living New York City. His favorite treats are Greenies.

rachel r. Rachel lives in New Jersey. Her favorite food is pizza. This is her first modeling assignment.

 sugar Sugar works with her person at The Woolgathering in New York City. You can visit her on the Upper East Side.

 tank Tank lives in New York City. In his next book, he would like to be photographed giving a "high five."

 wilder Wilder lives in Brooklyn. He enjoys long naps, pureed food, and being carried around the neighborhood.

 willow Willow is a six-year old Illision—a rare breed developing in the States and in Europe. She has mastered over 250 voice and hand signals.

 yeats Yeats is a wirehaired Fox Terrier who prefers a casual look. He has an extensive wardrobe. He loves to eat a snack from Alaska called Yummy Chummies (smoked salmon belly).

kate burton • *photographer* Kate Burton has been photographing children professionally since 1991. Her work has appeared in *Parents, Child, Time Out New York,* and *The New York Times,* who have called her photos "a work of art." She has exhibited in solo and group shows throughout the New York area.

lori gayle • *technical editor* Lori Gayle is a twenty-year veteran of the crafts industry and has worked as a professional weaver, knitter, and handcrafted clothing designer. She now works primarily as a technical editor for knitting books and magazines. A native New Englander, Lori lives in Massachusetts with her brilliant significant other, Chris (a British transplant), and a loud, feisty parrot named Keku. Although she does not currently have any babies or dogs to knit for, she is an enthusiastic fan of both.

Photo: Bill Manning

tara jon manning holds a masters of arts degree in apparel and textile design and fiber arts. Her design work can be seen in knitting magazines, books, and the collections of major yarn companies. A Crafts Yarn Council of America certified knitting instructor, Tara teaches from her private studio in Boulder, Colorado. She is also the author of *Men in Knits* and *Mindful Knitting*.